Defiant

A WICKED HEARTS STORY

SARA CATE

Defiant

www.saracatebooks.com

Give feedback on the book at:
info@saracatebooks.com

Printed in the U.S.A

Chapter One

RAFE

I'll give him this much, he's got a right hook that could knock my ass straight into next week. Which is exactly why I can't let him get that punch in. He's strong, but he's not very fast. Luckily for me, I'm a little bit of both.

Just as he comes in for a left, then a right, I move fast enough to miss his throws and use my momentum to sack a punch right into his jaw. I feel a shift under my fist right as it lands against his face. It's probably nothing, just a little crack in the hinge, but I bet it hurt like a mother fucker.

The pain makes him hesitate long enough for me to land another one on the other side. The crowd around us goes nuts. It's loud enough to distract me from the howling in my knuckles.

"Fuckin' pig," he growls before he comes in for another slow swing, which I block, and it brings him close enough to let me drive my fist into his rib cage. He stumbles, and this time I know I probably fractured something. And it feels fucking good.

I don't always want to hurt the guys I fight, but this one is a real piece of shit, so I take my pleasure where I can. He owns the strip club, the seedier one near the outskirts of town, and I've heard more than once that he's abusing his girls and making them work a little too hard for their money. Of course, none of them will come forward, and I can't get enough proof to shut him down. Until I do, cracking his ribs and breaking his nose is a goddamn delight.

He's only up long enough for me to bring a hard left across his cheekbone. Then he crumbles to the pavement like wet mud. The guys around me celebrate, and I know it's because they all just made some money on me. The few who bet against me stomp away cursing my name, but I have to turn a blind eye to that shit.

That's the deal.

It's part of the compromise I made with Vic, the owner of the gym. I can fight as much as I want. For him, I keep the cops away. Every time word gets out about a little illegal gambling behind the perfectly legal boxing gym, I shut the rumors down. For me, he lets me hang around these little concrete brawls, sniff around for leads if I need to, and we both stay happy. I don't make any arrests around here. I get to be a slightly crooked cop for a couple nights a week, and it pays off in bigger ways than shutting down some harmless betting.

Tonight, I'm here for more than just knocking out this slimy piece of shit finally coming to back his feet. And I see just the person I need to talk to. After I wipe off the sweat and blood dripping off my eyebrow, I head over.

As soon as I step up to her, Maggie rolls her eyes at me. "I'm not talkin' to no cop tonight, so just buzz the fuck off," she snaps at me, and a hearty laugh bubbles out of my chest.

"I can't even say hello?"

She presses her lips together, clearly not buying it for one second.

"Your nose is bleeding," she notes, but I know Maggie isn't grossed out by a little blood. As Vic's little sister, she's used to nights and crowds like these. She's easily as smart as him, twice as tough, and ten times prettier. And always good for a little intel.

Maggie is the wallflower. She's always around, but no one pays her any attmention. So she hears a lot.

"I'm not here to dig, Maggie. I just picked up a young kid yesterday for intent to distribute, and I want to know what the fuck I'm missing."

She averts her eyes and doesn't answer me. I take this to mean she knows exactly what I'm talking about. The kid's only sixteen, clean according to his blood sample, and was carrying twenty individually bagged grams of crystal. He kept his mouth shut, and I'd like to get other people talking before I pressure him to.

"Point me in the right direction, and I won't say another word."

"I heard about it, Rafe, but I honestly don't know anything. The guys are as confused as you are."

By the guys, she means her brother and his friends. The worst they do is a little underground fighting and gambling, but I know for a fact Vic hates drugs. He loves the fights, and he likes them to stay clean. I couldn't keep up our bargain if it were any other way.

Ever since I busted my club brother, Logan's supplier last spring, the narcotic activity around the beach has been quiet. A few little busts here and there, mostly punks who buy it in Newport and bring it to our little beach town. But this kid didn't come from Newport. His aunt and uncle own a souvenir shop on the main drag, and I have a very bad feeling that it's not just a bad habit he's picked up.

"He's just a kid, Maggie. A good kid."

Finally, she meets my eyes. "Unlike you and me, right?"

I swallow, wincing from the slowly building ache in my jaw. "Very unlike you and me."

"If I hear anything, I'll let you know. Vic hates it too, you know. Drugs fuck up his fights."

"Thanks, Maggie," I whisper, leaning in to plant a kiss on her cheek. She swats me away. I'm sure I smell awful.

As I walk back to the center of the crowd, I see a couple girls in the circle this time. There aren't many girls that fight, but man, the ones that do are fucking fierce. The blonde currently dominating is the only one who ever wins, and the guys fucking love these fights. I can't watch, mostly because she obliterates the poor girl who I assume is new at the gym, thinking she's tough and badass enough to take her skills to the parking lot. She's not. They never are.

Vic catches my eye, and I send him a subtle nod.

I've gotten about as much info as I'm going to get tonight, but fuck I don't want to go home. It's only midnight, I hardly have a black eye, and I'm still bursting with frustration.

When he sees me restless, he nods me over. I know where this is going. We do this dance every weekend. I fight a fair opponent and win.

He gives me someone a little bigger than me...and the outcome is usually less predictable. The gains for him are good. For me, I risk needing dental work or a trip to the ER, but at least I don't feel so restless or frustrated anymore.

"You sticking around tonight?" he asks, and I see the tall red-headed fuck I fought last week. I almost had him, but he nearly put his fist through my skull before I could land my last punch—at least that's what it felt like.

What are my choices? Go home alone? Logan and Murph are both cozy with their girls now, and I wasn't about to third wheel that shit. And getting knocked out was better than lying awake in bed all night.

"Yeah, fuck it."

SHELBY

Mr. Yan squeezes my hand while I take his blood pressure, and a smile creeps across my face. "You better relax or I'll be here all day."

"A dream come true for an old man like me."

"Oh, you don't want me hanging around here all day. Aren't you and Mrs. Yan watching the new 'This is Us' tonight?" I ask as I jot his numbers down on the chart. They're not worse than last week so I breathe a sigh of relief. I hate when the vital signs tell me the end is near and there's absolutely nothing I can do.

"Exactly," he laughs. "Don't leave."

"Oh come on," I answer. "That's a great show."

"She cries the whole time," he says with a roll of his eyes.

"Yeah...maybe Big Bang Theory instead. Something funny." Just then, the man's wife comes in. She's not all smiles like he is. It never ceases to amaze me the way the family reacts to the end compared to the patient. The family members hate me. I am the angel of death. By the time I show up, hope is lost, and my presence is just the cruel reminder they don't need.

"How is he?" she asks, interrupting our happy conversation.

"Numbers are looking good. Stable. At this point, no news is good news."

She doesn't seem pleased with this answer, and I see her lips tense into a thin line. It's not that they want their loved one to die, but the waiting is torture. Living in this awful hospice limbo has to be exhausting.

"I'll come back next week unless something comes up. You have my number." I turn to my patient. He doesn't like the bed the hospital delivered, so he's parked in his Lazyboy. I place a gentle hand on his arm. "Get to the crockpot scene in 'This is Us', then watch Big Bang."

"Nurse's orders," he says to his wife. She's wringing her hands, looking at me like she can't wait until I leave. And I get it. I'm in her house, but I want to see Mr. Yan smile one more time before I go, and when I look at him, he does.

No one tells you this part. The bond with your hospice patients is different. Stronger. And I never forget these smiles, not a single one. There's something about being the last person someone bonds with, the last new person in someone's life. It's a heavy honor to carry. And even though I've only been visiting the Yans for a month, I'm already dreading the end. I'll miss the way he squeezes my hand.

On my drive home, I keep the radio off. The silence is calming, and although the job doesn't send me spiralling like it used to, I still need this part—the unwind.

Rolling down the windows, I let this warm ocean breeze blow off the dust of sadness. Since moving to Wickett over the summer, I haven't spent a single day without driving with the windows down. It's a waste to do otherwise. The weather here is so much more temperant than in Newport. On hot days, the breeze is cool. On cool days, the sunshine is warm.

Just before I pull into the small grocery store parking lot, my phone rings, my brother's face showing up on the screen.

"Hello, Ezra," I answer, holding my phone up to my face.

"How's the new place?" he asks without greeting.

"You sound bitter." I laugh as I walk across the parking lot to where the carts are stored. "I love being out here, and we couldn't keep living together. It was killing your game."

"I have no game." He laughs.

"Exactly."

When Ezra and I moved out here, we started out in one apartment, but I knew that wouldn't last. I love my brother, but he suffocates me, constantly butting into my business. His guard is forever up, and he trusts no one, which means…dating for me is nonexistent.

So I recently got a place in the apartment complex near the coast. It's quaint, but when you can hear the ocean from your bedroom window, you don't need square footage.

"Just be careful. I know you work crazy hours and get home late. I just worry about you, that's all," he says. I can tell he's in the car by the sound on the line. He's been busy with work, doing pretty well for himself since he started running a souvenir shop on the boardwalk.

I don't blame my brother for his protective nature. Ever since Ezra got out of prison eight years ago, he's been different. It's like he's seen the worst of the worst, and it's all he can see now. It kills me to think of what it did to him, so I try to ease his worries when I can.

"If I learn some self-defense moves will you feel better?"

"Knowing how to throw a punch won't stop someone like a 9-mil."

We're not having this conversation. Not again. "My apartment is safe, well-lit, and I've seen a cop car parked out front a lot, so I think there's an officer living in the building. I'm not worried, and you shouldn't be either."

"Because cops are so trustworthy."

I pause. That was a stupid thing to bring up, and I should know better. Ezra hates cops...well one in particular, but it's a can of worms I hate to even open.

Before he can start on his tirade, I blurt out, "Ez, I'm at the store getting stuff for dinner. I gotta run."

"Okay," he sighs. "Get home before dark."

I say my goodbyes and hang up before he can drone on anymore. Without another thought in my mind, I pick up the ingredients for the only dinner I'll be having tonight: cheese, crackers, and wine. Then I hurry home because I have a date with my couch.

Chapter Two

RAFE

I couldn't drive home. That's for fucking sure. I can't see out of my right eye, and the bottle of vodka we opened after my big win didn't help. But at least I won. I got my ass kicked pretty hard, but a win's a win.

The gym is out by the railroad tracks, about twenty minutes from my apartment. The location sucks for actual business, but Vic has enough regular clientele—not to mention the under the table profits he makes, he doesn't struggle to stay open.

Dammit, the lights on the road are blinding.

The ride is silent as I sit in the passenger side of my own car with Vic behind the wheel. Shannon is following us in her car to take him back.

"You're too good to me," I groan as he pulls into the parking lot of my condo complex.

"Are you kidding?" He laughs. "You made me so much fucking money tonight."

"I didn't hear that," I grumble as I practically fall out of my car.

"Is he okay?" Shannon calls through the window of her car.

"I'm fine," I answer. "I just can't see through this pretty shiner." I toss her a charming smile that she rolls her eyes at and shakes her head. I try to conceal the way the ground tilts under my feet as they pull away.

That left hook hit my skull harder than I thought. How many untreated concussions can you get before it becomes a problem? I have a feeling it's not many.

As I stumble to the door, I notice the new car parked in the lot. Someone recently moved into the apartment next to mine, but I haven't seen my new neighbors yet. I work weird hours, so I don't expect to meet them at all. It's not like I'm bringing over a plate of cookies anytime soon. It's a single hallway with only two doors on either side of the elevator. The last guy who lived there got married and left...which is about as much as I could gather with our limited interaction.

All I can think about is the extra-strength aspirin and bourbon waiting for me on the kitchen counter.

That and my warm bed.

Tomorrow is my mandatory day off so at least I can sleep a little longer...hopefully not forever with the way my head is pounding.

These lights in the elevator are fucking ridiculous. Why are they so bright?

I love my apartment, even though I know I could save a lot of money by living a little farther from the water. I grew up on Wickett—or Wicked as it's been nicknamed over the years, but never with the sound of waves on my balcony. And I can afford it. So, why not?

When the elevator discards me on the fourth floor, I fish my keys out of my pocket just as the room starts swaying again. Fuck.

I'm just tired. That's all.

The keys fumble out of my hand before I can even get them near the keyhole. Sonofabitch. I can only stare at them for a moment because I know reaching down will only make my skull pound louder.

The sound of the door next to me opening registers as I bend down slowly. I pause, halfway down and peek under my arm to see a young woman in light blue scrubs coming out of her apartment. Her back is to me as she yawns and locks the door.

My fingers brush the keys, making her jump and turn toward me. Quickly, I grab them and stand up, watching her face as it comes into view.

No fucking way.

I know I hit my head hard, but I didn't hit it so hard that I'm now hallucinating, seeing a beautiful ghost from my past standing before me.

By the way she's glaring at me like a deer in headlights, the feeling is mutual.

This can't be happening. When did she come to Wicked? Why does she have to live right next to me? And where the fuck is that piece of shit brother of hers?

The moment stretches...as if seconds feel like hours. My vision starts to stretch too, and she becomes farther away, down a narrow tunnel, and I know I'm about to pass out.

"You're bleeding," she states before turning and disappearing into the elevator. Somehow I manage to keep together, and she's gone before everything goes black.

SHELBY

This can't be happening. It really can't.

On the short drive over to the Thomas house, where Mrs. Thomas has pulled out her IV again doing God only knows, my mind is reeling.

It was him...wasn't it?

Yes, it was definitely him. Sure, it's been almost ten years since we've seen each other, but there is no doubt in my mind. I wouldn't forget his face. Not in a hundred years.

Rafe goddamn Nolan.

Of all the apartments in this town, he has to live in mine...right next door?!

Maybe he doesn't live there...I say to myself, trying to find a situation in which my mind is not entering full panic mode. Maybe he was just dropping in on a booty call.

But no...that patrol car has been parked outside since I moved in. And I do know he's a cop now. I do know that much.

A few years back...on a whim and for no good reason at all, I did a little social media dig on him. I just wanted to know if he was struggling as much as Ezra was. He didn't have much on social media, but I did find him in the news, getting promoted to sergeant. I wanted to be sick.

Of course he was a cop. He certainly didn't hesitate to throw Ezra under the bus when he had the chance, and without any remorse at all.

The three of us graduated high school together in Newport. Rafe was out there for only the second half of his senior semester, but the three of us clicked immediately.

Our friendship carried after high school. I was doing classes at the community college while Rafe and Ezra were busy making stupid choices. Those two had their ideas...ways they could beat the system, get ahead, make a name for themselves.

I thought most of it was just talk. Until it wasn't.

Ezra spent two years in jail for it. Two years in jail alone. And now the man responsible was currently my next door neighbor.

The visit at the Thomas house only takes about five minutes. I'm in and out like a cat in the night. When I get back in the car, I notice it's almost four. It almost feels too late to try and sleep now. I'm up, so I might as well stay up.

Not like I could sleep with the way my mind is going a mile a minute. Can I even keep living in my apartment? I love it too much to leave, but can I even enjoy it now? Our balconies are next to each other. He can practically climb over into my room.

Ten years ago, I would have loved that. But now... now I'm thinking about taking Ezra up on his option to carry a weapon.

Right now, all I want to do is go inside, crawl back in bed, and listen to ocean waves, hoping for a few more minutes of sleep before the alarm goes off.

Coming off the elevator, I nearly scream when I see the heap on the floor next to my door. Rafe is lying, slumped against the door as he passed out there. For a moment, I think he might be dead...and what luck of mine if he were. But when I lean forward, I hear his breathing against the carpet.

I was gone for at least fifteen minutes. Has he been lying here that whole time?

He must be drunk. I noticed the way he stumbled picking up his keys. Which means I should just walk into my apartment and let him deal with his hangover on his own.

But that knot near his temple is worrisome. And it's bleeding. And the sudden scent of booze coming off of him is even more worrisome. Whatever he was doing before he came home tonight left him pretty banged up, and if he dies of a concussion on the floor outside my door, the cops will come asking me questions. What kind of nurse leaves a man for dead just because she thinks of him as the lowest scum of the earth?

Dammit.

It takes me a minute to roll him over and prop him up against the door, and I really hate to even touch him. He might as well be a stranger to me, and I strictly think of him that way while I peel open his eyelids to see the dilation in his pupils.

He starts to rouse when I do that. His eyes meet mine, and he flinches like I'm about to murder him with the cell phone in my hand.

"I think you have a concussion," I say without looking him in the eye.

"I'm fine," he growls, moving to stand.

"Good then," I answer, getting up and moving toward my door. If he said he was fine, then I'll sleep just fine. Even if he does die.

But he stumbles again when he gets to his feet,

reaching for the door handle like the world is turning sideways.

Oh, my God. He's really going to die if I don't do something.

Letting out a heavy breath, I turn toward him. "Let me help you, please. You clearly need it."

"I said I'm fine," he growls. He's struggling with his keys. It's painful to watch.

Without another word, I take them and put the one he's holding into the keyhole. He scowls at me as I turn it, and he steps inside. His shoulder slams into the wall and he lets out a curse.

No depth perception.

"You're drunk with a head injury, Rafe," I protest as he walks toward his kitchen counter. His apartment mirrors mine. Kitchen on the right instead of the left. Small studio living area straight ahead. He doesn't even bother to shut the door as he reaches for the prescription bottle on the counter.

"You should be careful what you take."

He doesn't answer, and I take a glance around. It's a single man's apartment alright. No decorations on the walls. Dirty dishes piled in the sink. Takeout boxes stacked on the counter.

Smells like cologne and cigar smoke.

"What did you do? Get in a fight with a vodka bottle or something?"

He laughs as he struggles with the childproof cap on the medicine.

"I thought I dreamed you, you know. When I passed out. I woke up and there you were...more like a nightmare," he mumbles so low I can barely hear.

I don't answer as I walk over and take the bottle out of his hands. Looking down at the label, my suspicions are confirmed: it's 325mg aspirin.

"You can't take this," I say as I look up at him. The blood at his hairline has dried and crusted along his scalp, and he smells awful.

"Watch me," he growls.

"I'm serious, Rafe. Aspirin is a blood thinner, and if you have a concussion, it could kill you."

"I'll take my chances."

My teeth grind together. Once upon a time, we were friends. Shit, once upon a time, we were more than friends. It's the only thing that makes walking into his apartment and giving him hell possible, but it still feels like I'm overstepping my boundaries. If he doesn't want my help, then I should just leave. At least I've given him medical advice, and if he dies, it's not on me.

"You didn't get these injuries on the job, did you?" I ask, still holding the bottle close enough to my body I know he won't try to take it back. "What kind of cop are you anyway?"

"Don't worry about it." He reaches for a glass off the counter and fills it with tap water, guzzling it down. When he finishes, he glares at me with his eyebrows creased together. "What the fuck are you doing here anyway? You stalking me or something?"

I roll my eyes. "I can guarantee my stalking skills would be put to much better use. Aren't cops supposed to be protecting people?"

"I do protect people."

"Do you?" I nod my head toward the swollen, broken skin of his right hand.

"I said don't worry about it."

With a shrug, I turn and walk toward the door.

"Hey, I need to take something for my head," he snaps at me.

"Well, you can't take this. It will kill you."

As I reach the door handle, I hear him let out a heavy sigh. "My head feels like it's being split in two, Shelby. Please."

My name coming out of his mouth sends chills down my spine. When was the last time I heard him say it? When was the last time I begged him to say it again just so I could press my mouth against his, loving the way his perfect lips looked as he formed the sounds.

Without a word, I turn around and head toward the refrigerator. I snatch the towel off the counter and fill it with ice, spinning it to hold the cubes in a single line. He watches me from the other side of the kitchen. Then I hand him the towel. "Drape this over your neck. It will draw the blood away from your head and ease some pain. Rest, but try not to fall asleep for at least another hour. Drink lots of fluids and if you feel like you're going to pass out again, call 9-1-1."

Then, without another word, I walk toward the door and leave his apartment.

Chapter Three

RAFE

My head is pounding only a little less today, but since the bitchy nurse next door stole my aspirin, I'm getting by on 500mg of Tylenol.

After sleeping half the day away, I head to the tattoo shop to check in on Logan and Murph. Since we've been popping more and more dealers lately, I've been feeling the responsibility to check on Logan more. Murph is keeping an eye on him too, but now that Logan has Sierra, I don't feel so worried about him getting hooked again.

When I get to the shop, Murph is leaning against the counter, his beefy inked up arms against the glass.

He doesn't greet me as much as give me a scowl.

"What the fuck happened to you?" he asks with a grimace.

"Good morning to you too."

The buzzing in the shop feels like knives being pressed into my ears. Logan and Savannah are both working at their stations, and they both pause to greet me. Savannah's round stomach hangs between her legs while she bends forward to finish the colorful owl on the client's arm. You almost wouldn't notice it unless she turned sideways. She smiles at me, but I know I make her nervous. Savannah is still self-conscious about how everything went down between her and Murph, but I'm not holding anything against her.

We all have fucked up pasts.

Speaking of...I nod Murph toward the backroom. When he meets me between the boxes of supplies and the worn out coffee maker, he grimaces at my face again. I know how bad it looks. My left eye is still swollen pretty bad, and it's hardly being hidden by the ballcap I have pulled down. I look like Brad Pitt in every scene of Fight Club...but worse.

"You need to stick to guys your own size," he says as he busies himself with unloading a box of supplies.

"How's Logan?" I ask, ignoring his advice.

"Better than ever. You need to relax. I told you I'd keep any eye on him."

I know he said that but we lost Logan's brother to an overdose, and he was using right under our noses without any of us knowing. I'm not going to bring it up though. I trust Murph, and he and Sierra are close enough that I know she'd talk to him if she was worried.

She's just another one of the girls that I know is more nervous around me than comfortable.

But she's good for Logan, so I'm not complaining.

"Hey, you remember when I went to Newport? Our senior year."

"Of high school?" Murph asks, pausing to think.

"Yeah. I got placed with that couple after the Hanson family kicked me out."

"I remember," he answers going back to what he's doing. His expression is harder now, and I know the memory isn't the best. The three of us were best friends back then. Theo, Murph, and me. Three foster kids with fucked up pasts...and pretty shitty presents too. Theo's little brother, Logan, and Murph's little foster brother, Ryder, were our little tagalongs, but it always came down to us.

Until I left...without any warning. Here one day... gone the next. Apparently, I'd exhausted every available home on Wicked so the only place I had left it go was an old couple in the city who were older and low on patience for unruly teenagers. It was either that or go back with dear old mom and dad...my real mom and dad...and that wasn't fucking happening.

I didn't return after graduation like I said I would, and that pissed Murph off. But in my defense...that was an easy thing to do.

"When you came back, you were different," he says, like he can read my mind.

Maybe that's what pissed him off.

"I went through a lot in those couple of years," I say, fixing myself a cup of coffee.

"Okay...why are you bringing it up now?"

I let out a sigh. This feels like twilight zone shit. I never thought I'd see these people again, and they just dropped onto my doorstep one night. Literally.

"Someone I knew from then...just became my new neighbor."

"An friend?" he asks, glaring at me with a head tilt as he cuts open another box.

"Fuck no."

"An enemy?" His hands freeze.

"Sort of."

"A woman?" His eyebrows jut upward as he asks.

I don't answer, just take a sip of the coffee, which is answer enough.

Murph doesn't respond, thankfully, but he goes back to what he was doing. I know girls for me is an awkward conversation. I'm not one to be public with my relationships, and I certainly don't date often. In fact, I don't think my friends have ever seen me with a girl at all. Not even once.

"It's not like that," I mumble. "Well...it was, but that was a long time ago. I have a little bit of...bad blood there."

"What kind of bad blood?" he asks, suddenly intrigued. Now he understands the reason I'm coming to him with this information. Murph and Logan and I don't have family. We have each other. When you're out in the world alone, you need to find your own tribe, the people who will back you up no matter what. And we all tend to find ourselves in sticky situations. I showed up for Logan over spring break and for Murph when things went down a few months back with Savannah.

I'd die for my brothers, and I know they'd do the same for me.

"I turned her brother in for something, and they never really forgave me for it."

"What did you—"

"I don't really want to get into it. I'm not proud of it, but the point is…they're suddenly back in my life, and I'm not sure I can trust them."

He stands up and walks over, placing a hand on my shoulder. "We've got you, Rafe."

"Thanks, man," I answer, finishing my coffee.

A customer walks in the door, making the bell ring as Murph goes out to greet them. I could be over exaggerating things here, but I'd rather be cautious than sorry.

SHELBY

"Get the fuck out of here," Ezra blurts out, staring at me wide eyed from the opposite side of his small living room. "This is insane."

He took my news about Rafe about as well as I expected him to. I stopped by on my lunch break between home visits, and I caught him on the phone with someone for work, but I could tell by his clipped tone and rushed goodbye that he's hiding something from me.

Which I expect. Ezra is a trouble magnet. Being good is too boring for him, and while he's been holding down this new business for a couple years now, I can tell he's up to something. I just have to figure out what it is.

"Tell me about it," I quip back over the salad I'm holding on my folded legs. I brought one for him too, but he hasn't touched it. He'll probably run through the drive through after I leave, but at least I tried. "I could not believe my eyes when I saw him standing in my hallway in the middle of the night."

"How long has it been?" he asks.

"Ten years. Exactly."

"Of course he's a crooked cop now." Ezra laughs.

"What makes you think he's crooked?"

"Where do you think he ended up with a concussion? Which he obviously didn't want medically treated. He probably beats up punks on the downlow or something."

That sounds pretty unlikely. Rafe was always a little harsh, rough around the edges, but he was never cruel. Then again, it's been a long time since I've seen him...so maybe he's changed.

"You know...I had a feeling we'd run into him here on the island. I always figured he'd come back...but I never thought you'd be living next door to him."

I choose to keep out the fact that I knew Rafe was at Wicked this whole time. I never wanted it to deter Ezra from moving out here to better himself. As far as I was concerned, it was water under the bridge. I knew my brother thought differently.

Talking to my brother is a delicate balance. He wants honesty, but he's so volatile, easily offended. Never takes responsibility for his actions. It makes things...precarious.

His expression falls as he leans forward, leaning his elbows on his knees.

"You okay?" I ask.

"I'm sorry," he mumbles, and I have to swallow down the emotion building in my throat. Ezra carries a lot of guilt where I'm concerned. Sorry I almost didn't make it through nursing school because I was on my own. Sorry I was dragged into his trouble. Sorry my life has revolved around him. Now sorry I'm living next door to the person he hates more than anyone.

Who we hate more than anyone.

"Ezra..."

"I know I've put you through a lot, Shel. And it feels like everything that's happened to us started with him, what he did to us."

I don't say anything. I've heard this before. How Ezra going to prison changed everything for us. How Rafe betrayed us.

"I'll never forgive him for as long as I live," he says, and I hear the emotion in his voice. "We trusted him, and he turned us in like it was nothing. I'll never trust anyone again because of that."

There are hairs to split in this conversation that I repeatedly choose not to. Like the fact that Rafe betrayed Ezra...not me. How Ezra wasn't exactly innocent, but somehow it's still Rafe who's expected to pay. I'm not defending Rafe. What he did was pretty awful, and I do still harbor all the hate in the world toward him for it, but Ezra is no angel.

"This is a new start for us, Ezra. Your business is going well, and we're happy here. Who cares if he lives next door? I never have to see him or talk to him if I don't want to. We can overcome this."

It's like my words don't even register in his ears because now he's looking at me like he's thinking hard about something, chewing the inside of his lip, contemplating.

It has me nervous as hell.

"I could move on if I knew we had closure. If I knew we served him what he deserves."

"What are you talking about?"

"Whatever he's into...whatever this is that brings him home at three in the morning as banged up as he was...if we had a way of figuring it out...we could turn him in for it. The ultimate retribution, Shelby."

"Ezra..."

He crosses the room and kneels next to me. "I'm not asking you to do anything you're not comfortable with. But it would be easy for you...to figure it out. Talk to him a little. Let him think the bad blood is behind us. Imagine how that would feel...to get back at him and know that we were not outsmarted."

Honestly...I couldn't care less about revenge or righting past wrongs. I don't care about Rafe one bit anymore, and serving him justice wouldn't help me sleep any better than I already do.

But Ezra. He's been living in the past. He's never moved on from his best friend breaking his heart and sending him to prison.

"I'll think about it, okay?" I touch his hand and see the moisture pooling in his eyes. My brother has always been intense, but it breaks my heart to see him struggling. "Until then, focus on work. Get out of this apartment. Go meet someone."

I pat his cheek and move to stand. "I need to get back to work."

"Thanks for coming over," he says, standing up and looking at me like he's disappointed.

"I promise I'll think about it."

Finally, he relaxes and smiles at me. "Of course,"

he says and wraps his arms around me for a hug.

When I leave Ezra's, I can't stop thinking about our conversation as I drive to my next appointment. I hate the way Rafe treated me last night. So rude, like I was imposing, helping to keep him alive. And he still has that arrogant attitude like nothing he does has consequences. I hated him after what happened before, but now. Now, I really hate him.

Chapter four

RAFE

That night I ward off the headache demons with a nice ambien-percocet-scotch cocktail. If the nurse bitch next door has a problem with that, she can go fuck herself. That little washcloth ice pack she made just isn't cutting it anymore.

Talking to Murph about Shelby and my time in Newport only seemed to stir up the memories a little bit more.

Shelby and I never officially dated, but I was a teenage boy and she was a beautiful girl. She and Ezra are twins, so we were all in the same grade and graduated together. They had a single mom, so they were on their own a lot too. Our time together was mostly the typical teen hangout stuff: getting high, wasting time.

I always looked at Shelby like she was better than us, but she stuck around anyway. She was smart. Mature. When Ezra and I wanted to nick a couple packs of cigarettes from the liquor store, Shelby just bought them for us instead. I would have never pursued a girl like Shelby. She was out of my league, but she came to me.

One night, I came over to pick up Ezra for a late night screening of the big horror flick at the time, and Shelby answered the door instead. Ezra had been called in to help his mom at her security job for the university, and I nearly walked away when she invited me in.

She made me something to eat since she knew I rarely ate with my foster family. She poured me a little cheap beer from the fridge, and after dinner we sat on the couch to watch TV.

If I closed my eyes, I could still hear the background noise and the smell of her perfume as she scooted a little closer to me. I could hear her voice as she whispered, "You know the reason I hang around Ezra so much is to be near you, right?"

It was the most beautiful sound, but I hated myself at that moment. I hated that she wanted me when she could have had anyone. Shelby and Ezra had no idea what my bio parents had done to me for years in my childhood. They had no idea that because of that abuse, I constantly wanted to put my fist through a wall anytime my mind ever came close to the idea of sex: a beautiful girl, a perky pair of tits, and especially the girl of my dreams leaning in to kiss me. I was a psychiatrist's wet dream when it came to mental issues.

Still, when she leaned in to kiss me, I kissed her back. She let out a little whimper as her body melted into mine, and it's a sound that haunts my dreams to this day.

When my dick started to react to her body, I pulled away. No fucking way I was bringing her into that shit.

That was the turning moment for me. Everything that happened between the three of us was born in that small kiss. Because I couldn't be in Shelby's life anymore. I couldn't bring her into my shit show.

When the cocktail doesn't do its fucking job, I roll over in bed and pull out my laptop. Curiosity has gotten the better of me, and I do a little search of Ezra's name first.

First thing that pops up is his mugshot and public record. He did four years for attempted robbery, but I knew that already. I click on his social media profile, and his current picture sends a little buzz of regret through my system. He's so grown now. Looking so much older than I remember him.

His current job lists a company called Hawthorne Wholesale and Manufacturing. I type the name in my search bar, and within minutes I see that this company doesn't manufacture shit. What they do is distribute cheap China-made products with some modifications and personalizations, like "Girls Weekend on Wicked" printed on bright pink T-shirts.

So, that's what brought him out to Wicked.

My tired mind suddenly remembers the kid I picked up this week who worked at the souvenir shop. I really hope those two are not related.

Moving past Ezra, I search up Shelby. Her profile is an open book. She's a hospice nurse. Not married. No kids. No travel. Just work and Ezra.

I still can't get over the fact that she just fell back into my life like it was nothing. I closed this chapter of my life years ago, and I'm not quite sure I want to ever reopen it.

Then a truly dangerous thought finds its way into mind...

If Ezra is involved with the shop where we picked up the kid, then it's possible he's involved in the new product floating around town. If that's the case, then getting close to Shelby would give me an easy in. She was always so close to her brother, I'd be an idiot to pass on the opportunity to learn more about him and his behavior lately.

It wouldn't take much. A little conversation. Maybe asking for forgiveness. Show her I've really moved on. I'm not the same man I was before. Build her trust and get where I need to be.

Then my heart cracks a little just thinking about what it was like pushing her away ten years ago. Could I handle that again?

Yes. It will be worth it to shut down the new dealer on the island. To keep my friends and Logan safe. It would definitely be worth it.

SHELBY

My back aches as I pull into the parking lot of the apartment building. It's past eight, and I haven't even eaten dinner. It seemed like everything came down at once this afternoon, and I never stopped for a second. All I want to do is eat, shower, and sleep.

God, I hope I don't get any emergency calls tonight.

I grab my bag out of the back and cross the parking lot when I see smoke billowing from the gazebo next to the door. It doesn't surprise me when I recognize the dark eyes watching me.

I pick up my pace, not wanting to deal with him and the sudden frequency we're seeing in each other lately. This better not be a habit.

Then, Ezra's words echo in my mind. It would be so easy for you to do it. You could learn so much, and he would trust you.

I didn't want revenge on Rafe then, but tonight

I'm feeling bitter. Anger courses through my veins. Work does that to me sometimes, especially when I lose a young patient...someone younger than me who shouldn't have to watch what it does to their loved ones. Life is just so fucking unfair sometimes, that I suddenly realize that if I can serve a little bit of justice in this life, I'm going to.

I pause near where he is sitting. He still looks just as handsome as he did when we were teens, if not more. He has dark hair and dark eyes, but there's a bright smile hidden under all the scowling that balances his features just right. I remember wanting to make him smile just to enjoy how beautiful it made him. Seeing Rafe smile was like looking directly at the sun.

"Are you hell bent on killing yourself?" I ask.

He smiles—a wicked, dark smile. Not the one I wanted, but he's still so handsome it makes me irritable. "Are you hell bent on stopping me?"

"It's my job," I point out, gesturing to the scrubs and badge hanging from my pocket. He nods, trying to show that he's impressed.

"I guess I should thank you then," he says with a grimace.

"How's your head?"

"Still hurts like a mother fucker, but I'm here."

"You know you really can't let something like that go untreated. You won't be so lucky next time," I say, hoisting my bag higher up on my shoulder.

"I really don't need the medical advice."

"I'm just trying to help," I argue. He stubs his cigarette out in the ashtray but doesn't move to walk inside. I should just leave, but he has me feeling irritated.

With a pointed stare, he says, "Well no one asked you."

Heaving a deep sigh, I turn toward the door. "Next time I'll just let you die."

Forgoing the elevator, I head straight for the stairs. I'm not in the mood to wait, and I'm still so high on rage that I could use the physical outlet. In fact, I know there's a gym in the basement that I bet has treadmills. Maybe a long jog would help to relieve the tension.

What is wrong with him? I helped him, in the middle of the night, and he's being a dick to me about it. I don't know when everything went wrong, why we went from friends to enemies in the first place. Everything was great, and it was like that one stupid kill all those years ago triggered something evil in him. It doesn't make any fucking sense.

Get over it!

When I reach my floor, I'm out of breath. From the exertion and the rage.

Pulling my keys out of my purse, I stop in front of my door, ready to be inside and safely tucked away, safe from him.

The elevator pings, and I grit my teeth. My fingers

fumble with the keys.

"Stop." His voice is low, commanding, and for some reason, I obey.

I literally cannot move as he stalks closer. I am completely frozen in place, way beyond my understanding, but I let him get so close I can smell the smoke on his clothes. He leans his elbow against the doorframe, settling close beside me, and although I can't move, I don't look at him. I keep my eyes trained on the keys in my hand.

He leans in and whispers harshly in my ear. "Listen, sweetheart, we are not friends. I have no desire to rehash old memories or bury any hatchet between us. I'm not looking for your forgiveness, nor do I want it. You helped me, and I showed my gratitude, but that's all you're getting out of me. I know your brother is still a fucking crook, and I take my job very fucking seriously, so I know the little game you're playing. Our friendship didn't stop me from turning him in then, and it won't stop me now."

At the mention of my brother, I flinch, turning up toward him with my lips pressed tight together. I have to hide the tremble in my lip as I stare into those dark abyss eyes.

I want to hurt him so badly at that moment, and it's a familiar desire that I hide from time to time: the craving to destroy something instead of fix it. The need to hurt someone instead of heal them. I have never hurt a soul in my life, but right now, I want to make Rafe Nolan feel pain. Then, I want him to die with it.

"Fuck you, Rafe," I snap at him as I finally find my key and turn the doorknob. He's still close behind me as I press into my apartment. Before I shut the door, I look him in the eye. "You can take your gratitude and shove it up your ass."

I slam the door in his face, and it doesn't fulfill this burning desire, but it does feel really good.

Chapter Five

RAFE

Why the fuck did I do that? I was supposed to be getting information about Ezra from her, and I just basically told her to fuck the fuck off forever. Something about her makes me crazy with rage. I don't want to be nice to her or help her or even thank her.

I want to watch her fight off tears like she did tonight. I want to see her cry. Drop on her knees and beg me for forgiveness. Then I want to deny her everything she wants.

What the fuck is wrong with me?

For some twisted reason, my dick is swelling up in my pants, and I squeeze my legs until the pain makes it stop. I need to get out some of this tension—and fast. Pacing around my apartment is not doing the trick so I grab my bag by the door and skip changing into my workout clothes.

As I leave my apartment, I choose the stairs over the elevator this time—like she did. Why, I don't know. Maybe for the same reason I'm going down to the gym, because I made her so mad she didn't know what to do with herself. I hope she doesn't sleep tonight because of it.

The gym is mine although technically anyone in the building can use it. I'm just the only one who does. Most of these rich assholes either have indoor spin bikes in their apartments or they run on the jogging paths by the water. Either way, I haven't seen another soul in here in years. So I took the liberty of making some adjustments. A large hanging punching bag hangs in the middle of the room, greeting me with the promise that I can abuse the shit out of it and feel a whole lot better when I leave here.

Quickly, I strip out of the button up shirt until I'm down to nothing but my jeans. Then, I ignore the subtle thud of pain in my skull as I start taking quick punches of the bag. The first few always feel the worst, but I fall into a rhythm after a few strikes.

I think about her taking my aspirin. Walking into my apartment. Choosing to live next to me when she could live anywhere.

I punch the bag thinking about her kissing me all

those years ago, fucking up every good thing I thought about her.

I think about the way her bottom lip quivered as I berated her and the way her eyes moistened when I threatened her about Ezra.

I punch the fear in her eyes. The hatred. The regret.

By the time I think about the way she froze in front of the door when I told her to, I'm breathless. Sweat drips from the top of my head, landing on my bare shoulders. My shoulders are crying in pain, and my head is now throbbing.

The tension is still lingering, like it always is, but it's not as bad as before. It's enough that I can pick up my shit and head upstairs. Hopefully this will help me sleep tonight because tomorrow I go back to work, which I sorely fucking need.

This little ritual of mine started when I was just a kid, when I had so much angst coursing through my body and no way to let it out that I found serving a good punch was downright therapeutic. Of course back then, I wasn't using punching bags. I spent a lot of time in detention and threatened to be kicked out of school. My precious mom and dad found this to be typical boy behavior, so they never really punished me for it. It was the other stuff they found repulsive. The more natural parts of being a growing boy that I spent hours repenting for, kneeling on thorns and taking baths so hot my skin blistered.

Thankfully, the child protective services frowned upon that kind of parenting and took me away when I was ten. The rest of my years were spent bouncing around from home to home with a dirty file filled with offenses and destined to only land in the homes that were less than welcoming.

But my parents would be thrilled to know I carried their penance with me all these years. I still need these punching bags and although I don't kneel on thorns anymore, I do find ways of torturing myself. I guess their methods truly fucking worked.

SHELBY

I can't get that asshole out of my head all day. Every single smile with every single patient is forced because I just hear his voice in my ear, his harsh commands that I obey, his pompous attitude like he's so much stronger and tougher than I am.

Thankfully, I only have one appointment after lunch, so I call into the office to let them know I'm taking the afternoon to catch up on sleep. They know I was working late last night, and I'm a liability at some point anyway. Of course, I don't catch up on sleep. I start browsing the internet, gleaning out every piece of information I can find on Rafe Nolan that is out there. I've already done the basic search, but now

I want to know more. I want to know everything so that I can use it against him.

Once I get through the basic buillshit from the precinct, I find some social media accounts that he's featured or tagged in. It takes me over an hour before I find a profile of a woman who works at Smokey's Bar on the boardwalk. She tagged Rafe in a couple of pictures, which means he must have had a profile at one time. He's looking pretty brooding in each of the pictures, until I get to one that makes my heart beat faster. She's kissing him.

It looks like they're at an event at the bar, and he's a few years younger. She's hanging on his shoulders, and he looks almost miserable. In a few of the pictures, he's smiling, but I can tell he's drunk in those.

The girl is pretty. She looks like the tough kind of pretty, the kind that comes with working around men and in bars. I bet she doesn't take shit and could drink me under the table. I guess you'd have to be tough to date Rafe.

I click on her profile and see that she still works at Smokey's. It's Thursday afternoon, and if I make the excuses in my head right, I can convince myself that I'm not stalking anyone. I'm just going out for a drink after a long week. Thursday's the new Friday, right?

I almost back out. Even after showering and putting on the nicest outfit in my closet—which is just a plain black skirt and flowery top I wear to every non-work event—I almost decide to check out a movie instead. Why do I even care about him? Why can't I just hate him in peace and move on with my life?

It was the way he talked to me last night, like he owned me. Like I belonged to him and was at his mercy to be treated like shit. That was the nail in the coffin for me. I want what Ezra wants now. I want to make sure that people like Rafe can't just walk around treating people like shit and get away with it.

All I'm going to do is find out something about him. It could be nothing or it could be useful. Maybe I'll find out what he does on his off hours that leaves him so beat up. Maybe I'll use it to turn him into the Chief of Police and have his rank taken away, bound to a desk or kicked off the force completely. Whatever he's dealt, he deserves it.

When I walk into the bar, it's still bright and quiet, which is actually a good thing. First, I notice a man behind the bar and disappointment washes over me. Then, a waitress passes by me, and I stop when I see her face.

"Hey, darlin'. Have a seat wherever you'd like. Kitchen is open." She hands me a menu, and I can only focus on her bright smile and tan, toned shoulders. She's even prettier in person, and I feel entirely inadequate in her presence.

"Thank you," I mutter as I take the menu and walk toward the bar. The man washing dishes heads toward the back and the waitress with her name, Laini, printed on her nametag greets me.

"What can I get for you to drink?" she asks, and I fumble with my thoughts before I finally blurt out, "Titos with soda and lime."

She smiles at me and winks.

"Good choice."

I feel her watching me while she prepares my drink. "Meeting somebody?" she asks.

"Umm…no," I stammer. I'm a terrible liar normally. I hate lying. It makes me feel so exposed and vulnerable, but I suddenly pull out some random inspiration. "Long week. Needed a good drink."

"Gotcha. What do you do?" she asks.

"I'm a hospice nurse," I answer without thinking. I'm not comfortable coming up with a fake name and job. Besides, this is a small town. A lie that big would definitely come back to haunt me.

"Oh," she says, looking impressed. "Well then, this one is on the house. Nurses should always drink for free."

"Thank you," I smile, and for a moment, I don't want to do this. I like her. She's down to earth, and if she's already been through dating Rafe, she hardly needs some jilted nurse coming in to give her hell. And she's probably not going to like rehashing those old memories at all.

But I do it anyway. As I take my first sip, I squint my eyes at her and she pauses. "I'm sorry. It's just…you look so familiar!" I say, staring at her with as genuine an expression as I can muster.

"Well, I've been tending bar here for ten years, so maybe that's it."

"I'm actually new to town," I say, still staring at her face. "You know what it is," I laugh. "I think I saw you on Facebook. I think you used to date a friend of mine."

So far none of this is a lie, I tell myself. Well, except for the friend part.

Her face breaks out in a shocked laugh. "Oh God, which one?"

"Rafe Nolan," I say carefully. It feels like an explosive device, like his name alone can detonate and ruin all the joy and happiness in this room.

Her smile fades and she plants her elbows on the bar across from me. "Oh, Rafe," she sighs. "Jesus, I haven't thought of him in years. How is he?"

I see the searching expression on her face, like she's scanning her memory, untapping old moments in time that she locked up a long time ago. I'm almost sorry about it.

"Ah, you know...same old Rafe," I say with an easy, laidback tone.

She lets out an uncomfortable laugh. "How do you know him?"

"We graduated high school together, actually. Now we're neighbors." Still not a lie.

"Oh wow. Yeah...Rafe..." she heaves a long sigh just saying his name. Goddamn, what did he do to her? "That was a long time ago."

Just when I finish my drink, she gestures to it and I nod, placing my empty glass on the rubber mat at the edge of the bar. When she walks back with a fresh drink, she eyes me skeptically for a moment, and I'm afraid she's caught me, like she could somehow tell I'm actually spying on my worst enemy instead of chatting about a mutual friend.

"You didn't date him, did you?" she asks.

"Oh," I say with shock on my face. "No. We were just friends, but I know how Rafe is…he's a little…"

I let my words trail, hoping she'll finish it for me. After a long, agonizing moment she leans in and says, "Intense?"

"Yes!" I blurt out. The vodka is hitting me, and I'm feeling loose, relaxed. "Intense is right."

She laughs, and once again, I'm admiring her easy-going nature. I hate that I'm using her when I'd like to actually get to know her. Maybe come in here every Thursday, build a relationship until we start catching movies or hanging out together.

Goddamn. It's obvious I really need to start socializing more. I need to make actual friends or I'm going to end up like the asshole next door.

"Well, intense could be a good thing, right?" I ask with a wink, my drink straw held between my lips.

Laini laughs again. "Girl, there is such a thing as too intense. The thing about Rafe was, and I'm sure you know this about him, he was dealing with so much emotional baggage that he just wouldn't unpack so he was walking around like a ticking time bomb."

A hesitant chuckle escapes my lips. It's unnerving to hear a complete stranger talking about someone I used to know so well. "You hit the nail on the head there." Then, I lean in, as if the few other drunk older men in the bar give half a shit what we're talking about. "I was always curious about him...what he's like, you know, in that aspect."

She makes a few wordless expressions with her eyes. "Well, I don't know about that either. Rafe wasn't..." She leans back and stops herself. "I shouldn't tell you that part, but I will just say this... That man is waging wars in his head, and the bedroom is his battlefield."

Holy shit.

I nearly suck down the rest of my second drink in one slurp as she walks away to help another customer. I'm stuck on a few pieces of her last statement. One: What part was she not comfortable telling me? Is he into some strange kink that she doesn't want to share? Two: What the hell does she mean about the bedroom being his battleground? Is he as cruel and abusive in bed as he is in person?

I'd be willing to bet.

And still...I find myself shifting in my seat just thinking about it.

Okay, that's definitely a sign I've had too much to drink. Just then, she places another one in front of me.

"This is from the gentleman at the end of the bar," she says and with her back to him, she nods her head until I make eye contact with a wiry, blond man with a fake smile and an expensive-looking watch on his wrist.

"Oh, thank you," I mumble. When I look up at Laini, she just gives me a wide-eyed look that says 'do not engage,' and I take the advice.

"Then talk to me so I don't have to go over there," I mutter.

She laughs and leans on the bar again. "I like you. What's a girl like you doing hanging out with Rafe?"

"I told you. Old high school friends, now neighbors."

She nods her head. "Be careful with that one. He's damaged, but there's a soft side under all those scars."

I swallow, pushing away the thought of a soft side to Rafe. That doesn't exist. Not for me anyway.

When she stands up, she says over her shoulder while pouring a beer, "Hey, is he still fighting at Vic's?"

I freeze, wracking my brain for a response. Vic's? Fighting? What does that even mean? Like MMA or something?

Then, my brain connects the dots, and I remember the concussion and bleeding eyebrow. It makes total sense. "Oh, yeah," I announce. "He does."

A voice from across the bar adds in, "Oh there's a big lot fight at Vic's tonight," he says. I nod at the man who bought me the drink.

"What's a lot fight?" I ask, looking at Laini.

She gives a roll of her eyes toward the guy who brought it up. "It's their less-than-legal fighting match that takes place in the lot behind the gym on most nights."

"If you like making money, it's a great place to win a bet. I'd be happy to show you who to put your money on." The man smiles at me, and I force a weird, uneasy grin on my face.

"No, thanks." I smile. "Not really my scene."

"Rafe wouldn't be there, though," I say to Laini. "If it's illegal."

She laughs at me, placing my tab on the bar. "You don't know him as well as you thought you did."

She's not wrong there. I guess there was less lying than I expected there to be tonight.

I look down at my phone and see it's now almost seven, and it's starting to get dark outside. Quickly, I type Vic's into the search bar on my maps app and see it's about a fifteen minute drive, which is too far for me to be travelling after three drinks.

I can't seriously be considering this. I have no place visiting an underground fighting ring on a Thursday night by myself.

But before I know it, I'm ordering myself a ride and paying my tab at Smokey's.

Chapter Six

RAFE

Initially, I came out to Vic's as a spectator. It's a big fight night at the gym, and most of the evening is legal and takes place inside. I have nothing against fighting with regulations and a softer floor to land on, but I don't have the time to actually train and put in the hours these regular fighters do.

So when I come to the gym tonight, I do it without any premeditated goals in mind. I'm not looking into anything or trying to question anyone. And I'm not fighting. My head is still a mess from a couple days ago, and as much as I hate to take advice from that know-it-all stuck up princess next door, I probably should avoid any more brain shakers for a while.

The fights are good entertainment, but I still can't keep Shelby out of my head. I was in the basement all night trying to punch the edge off. Something about her just walking into my life to fuck everything up for me just gets my blood going.

Vic finds me hoving near the corner of the crowd just before the last fight is about to start.

"We got you on the books tonight?" he asks without greeting.

"Not tonight. I can't risk taking any more hits this week." I gesture to my still black and blue left side.

"Ah, with these guys I have tonight, you won't be taking any hits. Promise."

Of course, I don't take a cut of the winnings, so he loves when I fight. Not to mention, it draws a crowd. People love watching a cop acting like a regular asshole when they're off the clock.

"I'll think about it," I answer without looking at him.

Vic exhales next to me, and I know he doesn't like someone else calling any shots at his gym, but I'm not going to just bow down and fight whenever he wants. I have to keep him in his place. I already know I'll do it, but he doesn't.

He walks away, taking his pissed off attitude with him, and I settle in to watch the last regulation fight of the night.

Before the last bell rings, the crowd has started

oozing out into the parking lot behind the gym, ready for the real fun to start. The security at the gym keeps that crowd limited to legit gamblers and people they trust not to fuck it up.

And I'm about to follow them out there when someone across the room catches my attention. It's not just that she's a woman in a predominantly male room, it's that she's alone, and she's the one fucking person I came here to forget.

I'm trying to wrap my head around why Shelby is standing near the stands, looking around like she's trying to find someone. You've got to be fucking kidding me, right now. What the hell do I have to do to get this girl out of my life? I literally can't get away from her. It's just not right, goddammit.

I glare at her with a tight-lipped expression and hard eyes as I wait for her wandering gaze to land on me. When it finally does, my nostrils flare and I make my way across the stands to meet her on the other side. So I can promptly send her ass home.

As she stands near the front of the room waiting for me, I notice the way she's dressed. Nicer than usual. She's not in her scrubs, but she's too fucking fancy for a place like this. She looks like she should be at the Cheesecake Factory, not here.

When I get closer, I notice that the color of her eyes pop thanks to a thick layer of makeup and longer than normal lashes. Is she trying to draw attention to herself?

"What the fuck?" I ask as soon as I step up to her.

"What?" she asks, squaring her shoulders and trying to look proud.

"Go home," I snap, not even bothering to ask why she's here. There can't be a reason good enough. Then I catch a whiff of the vodka on her breath. "Tell me you didn't just drive out here."

"I'm a grown woman, Rafe. I can go wherever I want and get there safely, thank you."

Just then, the bell rings and the crowd erupts. The fight is over.

"Well, you missed the events, so you should call your ride back."

I take her by the back of the arm and steer her toward the exit. Of course, she fights back, trying to snake her arm away, but I just lean in and put my lips next to her ear. "Stop it."

Suddenly, she stills and looks at me with a wide-eyed expression, like even she can't believe that shit works.

"Nolan!" a familiar voice calls from behind me. Fuck. I know that voice even before I turn around.

Vic is approaching, and he has a subtle smirk on his face as his eyes zero in on Shelby standing all doe-eyed and innocent as fuck.

He doesn't say anything for a moment, but the smile he aims at her sends chills down my spine. "Who's your friend?" he asks. I watch his gaze cascade down her shirt to her skirt and then her legs.

"Shelby," she answers with a demure smile as he takes her hand, kissing her knuckles gently.

"She was just leaving," I mutter, turning Shelby toward the door.

She pulls away from me, and I swear I'm about to toss her over my shoulder and throw her in a cab.

Vic grins at me, and it's grating on my nerves. "Now, now...the fun is just getting started," he laughs.

"I just came to see the fights," Shelby says, and the subtle slur to her words proves my theory correct. She's been drinking.

"Rafe invited you?"

"No," she says like that would be so terrible. "I was at a bar in town and someone mentioned the fights, so I wanted to see it for myself."

"Oh really?" Vic asks with a smile. "So, how do you know Rafe?"

She glances up at me as if she's looking for help in answering that question. "He's my neighbor," she answers coolly.

"I'll walk you to your car," I say, trying to push her toward the exit again.

"I want to stay," she growls at me, and Vic steps in, taking her arm with his.

"You don't want her to miss the best part," he croons as he guides her toward the back door that leads to the parking lot brawls. My shoulders start to tense, and my molars couldn't possibly grind together any more.

I have half the mind to just bail at that point. I couldn't give two shits what happens to her if she stays, but with the way Vic was eye-fucking her, she would have a hard time getting out of here alone. She's not my goddamn responsibility anyway, and she brought herself here, so she can get herself out of here.

The exit is calling me, and the only reason I don't walk through that door is because now I want to punch something—or someone, really fucking hard.

SHELBY

The vodka is wearing off, but Vic's attention on me is my new form of intoxication. He's downright the sexiest fucking man I've ever met—tall, dark, and handsome, as they say. He towers above me, and all of the darkness is in his eyes and demeanor. Vic looks like the kind of guy who people bow down to...for different reasons, of course.

With his jet black hair slicked back he smiles down at me, and for a man like Vic, getting a smile feels special. His hand rests on my lower back as he guides me back to a raised deck behind the gym. There are already a group of men sitting around the table with paper and pencils, and it sounds like they're discussing the lineup.

"So, Shelby, tell me what you do for a living," he says. His voice is deep and sexy, and I'm so lost in those cool, dark eyes that I can barely remember my name, let alone my occupation.

"I'm a hospice nurse," I say with a shake in my voice.

He gives me an expression that seems like he's impressed. He pulls out a seat for me, and it's nothing more than a patio chair, but Vic has a presence about him. He may not be some big mob king, but around here, he's treated like royalty.

"I hope this kind of stuff doesn't bother you, then," he laughs, sitting in the seat next to me. He puts his arm across the back of my chair and leans in.

"Not at all," I answer. Which is true. "Maybe it was growing up with a brother, but I also love action movies and violence." He laughs, and I feel his fingers graze my shoulder. Vic is laying on the moves. I'm not sure how I feel about it yet.

There's a large crowd milling around the parking lot. We're far enough away from any place where people could see or hear the crowd back here. Lights overhead illuminate the center where a chalk circle is drawn. Across the circle, I notice a familiar, brooding face watching me.

I actually thought he would leave once I walked off with Vic, but it looks like he stuck around to stink face me the rest of the night. Which is fine. All the more opportunity to find out more about him while I flirt with the gym owner. Rafe clearly wanted me to leave when he saw me here, and I just love doing whatever makes him angry.

"So, I have to know," I say with a smile, leaning toward Vic. "Does Rafe really fight back here?"

Vic puts on a little display like he's surprised I asked that and is trying to decide how much he can tell me. It's all a flirtatious show. Finally, he leans in and puts his arm around my back. "Officer Nolan and I have a mutual agreement. I keep the fights clean and no one gets hurt. And of course, no gambling," he adds in with an adorably fake serious expression. We all know that last part is utter bullshit. The only reason he would do this at all is for the money, and I can clearly hear the guys behind me taking bets, even though I think they're trying to be in cognito about it.

"And what does he get in return?" I ask, genuinely curious.

With a shrug of his shoulders, he says, "He gets to let off some steam. Socialize. Get out for a little bit."

Something about that doesn't sound entirely believable. I have a feeling there is more involved than he's saying.

Just then I hear Rafe's name being said behind me. I turn toward the guys at the table.

"Yeah, we have Rafe and Mac on for ten," a young guy with a tattoo creeping up his neck mumbles before listing a few more names that I don't catch because I'm still stuck on Rafe's.

"Did they just say Rafe is fighting?" I ask Vic, who turns around to the guys.

"Nah, Rafe said he was out tonight."

"No, he told me he's up," the red-headed man at the table says, looking at his paper.

"He can't," I blurt out. Vic looks at me in surprise. I almost say something about his concussion but decide to bite my tongue. If Vic knows Rafe is leaving here with major injuries, or is at least telling people about it, it could cause more problems than I want to solve at the moment.

"Excuse me for a moment," I say as I get up to stand, but before I can leave, a hand lands on my forearm.

"Now, wait a minute," Vic says with a saccharine sweet smile. "He's a grown up. If he wants to play, he can play. He doesn't need his mama telling on him."

There's a serious undercurrent in his tone, and I sit back down, feeling suddenly a little more nervous than I was a moment ago. Vic may put on a sweet face for me, but I'm willing to bet he has a lot of money riding on these fights, and if I get in the way of that, he could lose his good disposition.

Suddenly, I pick up all the chatter around me. I can't find his face across the crowd anymore. All I can think is that if he gets one bad punch to the head, he could be riding out of here in an ambulance. Does Vic even let the ambulance come out here? What happens when someone gets seriously hurt? He says it doesn't happen, but I'm not buying it.

Now, I wish more than anything I was back in my apartment and that I hadn't come out at all.

Just then, a man in the center of the circle starts speaking loud enough for the crowd to quiet down. I spot a man off to the left. He's a younger man with blonde haired slicked back and sculpted shoulders. I bet he could throw a punch strong enough to knock someone out.

On the other side of the circle, I spot Rafe. He's shirtless, and I'm surprised to see that he is also heavily sculpted, thick cords of muscle cascading down his chest. He has black tattoos across his chest and back that are too far away and too intricate to make out from here. He didn't have those back in Newport, and I get lost for a moment just staring at his body. He's wrapping his hand in gauze, sizing up his competition with a blank, cold expression.

Holy shit. That look in his eyes says he's ready to kill someone. Jesus, I hope no one actually dies out here.

The announcer calls some arbitrary rules and taps each guy's shoulder. The whole thing feels so rushed, and by the way the crowd goes wild, I can tell these spectators just want fighting, as much and as fast as they can get it.

"Best seats in the house," Vic says into my ear. We're sitting on a deck a couple feet off the ground giving us a good view over everyone else's heads.

Within the first ten seconds of the fight, the opponent throws a punch toward Rafe's head, which makes me scream. Rafe dodges the throw easily and lands a quick jab to the other guy's cheek.

At first, I hate it. The sound of their bare fists hitting each other's faces is awful, but then the crowd yells and the adrenaline kicks, which I can imagine is even more intense for the fighters.

Rafe manages to dodge swing after swing and get in a couple punches that make contact. The other guy starts staggering on his feet, and I can barely breathe with anticipation for it to be over.

Then, Rafe hesitates just once. He doesn't lean back fast enough and he gets a set of knuckles straight to his jaw. I let out another scream.

I shouldn't be worried about it. After the way he's been treating me, I know I should be rooting for the other guy. I should enjoy the sound of the blond guy's punch hitting Rafe's face, but my fists clench as I wait for Rafe to throw another swing.

Rafe backs away and the other guy follows. When I try to move toward the circle again, Vic grabs my arm. I'm torn. I want to see the next hit, and I want it to be over.

"Just watch," Vic says to me, and his voice is reassuring.

Rafe lets the guy corner him, but when the opponent tries to swing again, Rafe slides to the side effortlessly and delivers a crushing blow to the other guy's face, sending him to the ground.

My hands fly to my mouth, and I stand there horrified as I watch the announcer crown Rafe the winner. I don't move for a long moment before Vic pulls me in for a side hug. "I hope you'll join us again," he whispers to me. Then he just turns away and settles business with the guys at the table.

Without him at my side, I rush off the patio and run toward Rafe. When I find him walking toward the edge of the lot, I send a hard slug to his arm. He's still shirtless, so my hand meets the cool sweat of his skin.

"What the hell?" he cries.

"What is wrong with you? You could have been killed!" I yell.

"Why the fuck do you care?" he growls as he continues walking. He's unwrapping the gauze from his hand, and it's bleeding like hell so the once-white cloth is now dark red.

"Why do you hate me so much?" I yell.

"Hate you? That's where you've got it all wrong, Shelby. I don't hate you. I just don't give a shit about you." He winces and tries to shake out his hand. "Fuck," he mutters and looks down at it.

I try to feel the hurt from his words, but they don't hurt, and maybe what he's saying rings true for me because I don't care that he doesn't care about me. I don't care about him either.

I'm doing this for Ezra, I remind myself.

"Let me look at it," I bark at him, reaching for his bloody hand. Stopping him under one of the lights, I see the lacerated skin along his knuckles. He should have stitches, but I have a feeling that's out of the question for him. He'll settle for some bandages.

"Well, I know that you weren't going to fight to-night. Then all of a sudden you decided to...maybe because I showed up."

"Don't be stupid," he snaps. "Vic asked me to fight."

"Whatever," I answer, tired of fighting. "You need something on these cuts. I have a bag in my car," I say, but one look at the parking lot reminds me I didn't park here because I didn't drive here. "Fuck."

"Let me guess. You don't have a car and you need a ride home," he says with a furrowed brow.

I don't answer but give him an uneasy expression. He rolls his eyes before turning away from me and walking toward the lot.

"Lucky for you, I brought my bike tonight. Let's go."

Chapter Seven

RAFE

With her arms around me, we sail through the darkness, the cool breeze in my face. The drive is quiet out here, and I like it that way. It gives me time to just think.

Normally I think about cases at work, but tonight I keep replaying the days back in Newport between me and Shelby. I try to remember how I felt about her then. It's not like thinking of a memory, but feeling it. And the memory of her felt comfortable, like Shelby was the closest thing I had to something nurturing in my life.

It doesn't line up with the feeling I have toward

her now. Now, Shelby represents this new sense of frustration and chaos. My lifestyle demands control. At work, at the gym, with the guys—I need to maintain control at all times. Shelby is...completely out of control. She shows up when I least want her to, out of nowhere, and she doesn't listen to me.

Except of course for a couple of times I've noticed the way she bends, stopping herself when I tell her to. As if she doesn't want to listen to me, but she has no choice.

I wanted to keep her around to get information on her brother, but at this point, it's not worth it. She's weaseling her way back into my head, and I can't fucking think straight. I need her out of my life, immediately.

As we pull into my parking spot, she climbs off the bike and waits for me. It's past midnight now, and my exhaustion is suddenly overwhelming. It's been a sleepless week.

"Please let me look at your head inside," she begs.

"I'm fine. Will you stop trying to take care of me all the goddamn time?" I answer, stomping across the lot toward the building.

"What the hell is wrong with you?" she snaps from behind me, but I ignore her as I reach the elevator. She's standing next to me when it opens. "I've been nothing but kind to you, and you're always an asshole to me."

My molars grind as we walk into the elevator together, and as soon as the doors close, I spin on her, glaring down with rage in my eyes. "Bullshit," I snap, and her face pales. "You're not being kind to me. I know you have that manipulative brother of yours in your ear all the time. I wouldn't be surprised if he planted you right next door to me just so he can keep tabs on me. Is he plotting his revenge? Does he just want to torture me for eternity with you showing up everywhere I turn?"

I watch as her eyes glisten with moisture and her breathing gets shallow. I don't care if I hurt her feelings. Shelby makes everything in my life difficult, and the sooner I scare her away, the better.

I expect her to keep quiet as I get off the lift and head toward my apartment, but she stops me in the hallway as she yells after me. "You turned your back on us, Rafe. We were supposed to trust you, and you turned your back on us." The sweet tone of her voice is gone, replaced with the husky sound of oncoming tears, exhaustion, and anger.

But she's picked a fight, and I don't back down from a fight. Turning back, I point a finger right in her face. "No, Shelby. I turned my back on him. Not you."

"He's my family, Rafe!"

"Yeah, well you were mine." The words spill out of my mouth on the adrenaline express. It's been a long fucking day, and I cetainly didn't mean to admit something like that, but neither did she because she's staring at me with wide eyes and her mouth hanging open.

"But that was a long fucking time ago," I growl as I turn toward my door.

"I thought you hated me..." she whispers, suddenly standing right behind me.

"Go to bed, Shelby."

"After that kiss that night, you never spoke to me again. Why didn't you say something?" she begs, while I'm fumbling with my goddamn keys again. I really needed to either stop locking it so I can get away from her quickly or get more organized with my keys because this shit just keeps happening.

"Will you fucking drop it?" I bark at her. The next thing I know the soft skin of her hand is on my arm and I snap. Spinning toward her, I knock her arm away and push her body against the door, trapping her and forcing her face even closer to mine. Her eyes are wide with fear which melts quickly to something else as I loosen my grip on her neck.

"Fuck," I mumble, inching away. "I'm sorry...just don't touch me, and please just fucking dop it."

"I'm sorry," she breathes, but my hand is still around her throat, a loose grip as I feel her pulse thrumming under my fingers. I realize the look in her eye, the one that's no longer fear, is lust. Her full, pink lips are parted, and she's staring at me through hooded lashes with her chest held out toward me.

It's doing things to my head.

Our eyes remain locked, and when she licks her lips, I pick up every little sign like I'm a goddamn satellite tower. She's not fighting me, and she sure as fuck doesn't look scared of me anymore. Like putty in my hands, I realize she's mine to play with. She wants to get into my head. It's my turn to get into hers.

SHELBY

A moment ago, he had my body slammed up against this door like I was under arrest, and at the moment, I'd let him cuff me if he wanted to. Maybe it's the current dry spell I'm under or maybe it's all the intensity between us, but my body is blazing hot under his touch.

I hate his smug attitude and his cruel tone. I hate the way he talks to me and the way he treats me. I hate everything about him, but right now, I'd let him lift my skirt and have his way with me.

He's certainly not having trouble picking up the vibe I'm putting out there because instead of letting go of my throat, he leans in. His breath is on my cheeks as his other hand trails a feather-light pathway down my body.

"Hands behind your back," he growls, his voice so deep it sends chills down my spine. Without hesitation, I obey and shove my hands between my body and the door.

Instantly, I'm turned on even more. The feeling

of being so vulnerable, with my body exposed to his touch makes me shiver with excitement. I've never really been into the tied-up stuff, but already I can see the appeal. My heart is hammering in my chest.

His hand floats away from my throat and he places it against the door, caging me in. His lips close in on the space beneath my ear, but instead of kissing me, he takes a gentle bite of my skin. Moisture pools between my legs.

When I feel the rough grip of his other hand on my hip, I realize that I'm putting myself in the hands of my own enemy. No matter what he said about me being his family, the love between us is gone. He's being a little rough on purpose, bringing me just enough pain to remind me that he hates me. Somehow, that realization only intensifies my arousal. It's like I want him to hurt me.

A high-pitched whine escapes my lips when I feel his cool breath on the wet skin of my neck. My hands stay obediently behind my back, even when he lifts my knee to position himself between my legs, grinding his hips roughly against mine.

He still hasn't kissed me, but he keeps up the nibbling on my neck and the rough pinches of the flesh of my ass. My mind is screaming at me to wake up and realize that he's only teasing me. He's fucking with my head, but my body refuses to listen. Currently, my body is willing to shed these clothes, drop to my knees, and let him be as rough as he wants to be. In fact, I'm pretty open to him being as rough as he can be—which is the first time I've ever felt like that.

"Let's go in my apartment," I say in a pant, but he doesn't respond. The hand he held planted against the door slides down, over my shoulder and brushes my breast over my thin shirt. It doesn't stop as he reaches the hem and snakes his fingers underneath. Feeling his skin against mine makes me gasp, and I wait for his reaction when he finds out that this backless blouse does not allow for a bra.

Trailing his fingers upward, he reaches my breast and pounces, grinding his hips against me harder as he squeezes my flesh, like an animal feasting on its prey. Suddenly, my shirt is up over my tits, and his lips leave my neck to devour the taut pink buds of my nipples.

I'm pretty sure I just came a little in my panties.

If he doesn't pull me into one of these apartments and fuck me senseless, I'm going to lose my mind. I've never wanted hate sex so much in my life.

"Rafe," I beg, my voice husky and lust filled. "Let's go into my apartment."

He switches to the other breast without an answer, and I let out another moan. Tilting my hips up toward him, I try to maneuver myself against him at just the right angle. If he's not going to fuck me, then at least maybe I can get some friction.

But it all becomes too much, and my wrists ache from being pinched between my body and the door, so I pull them out and reach for his belt buckle. At this point, I'm not above doing it in the hallway. Everyone's asleep anyway.

As soon as my fingers touch his pants, he pulls away, glaring at me like I've offended him.

"You broke the rules, sweetheart," he growls at me, his head tilts down so he's watching me through a hooded brow.

"What?" I breathe, but before I can move, he's putting the key into his lock and disappearing into his apartment.

"Goodnight," he says in a teasing tone before the door slams.

What. The. Fuck.

My body is still buzzing, but it's gone cold from the emptiness where there was just human contact. He was fuckign with me, I know it.

Instead of going into my apartment, I turn to his and bang my fist against the surface.

"You're a real asshole!" I shout. "You think you're so fucking tough and cool, but I think you're just lonely and pathetic, and I'm glad I didn't fuck you!" He doesn't answer, and I don't feel better yet. The lust has turned into rage.

"I'm sure I'm better off by myself anyway! At least I know I'll get the job done!" I shout just as a door down the hall opens and an old woman in a bathrobe peaks her head out.

"Shut up!" she wails at me, and I throw an apologetic hand up toward her before rushing into my place.

I lay in bed that night tossing and turning. Unfortunately, I was wrong, and no matter how hard I try, I just can't get the job done. I can't even get myself there because I'm too much in my head now, hating him and thinking of things I want to tell him.

Growing tired and irritated, I know I won't sleep until I take care of myself, so I imagine my hands tied behind my back, his fist in my hair as he pulls it and growls in my ear. I hate that it's the image of him that finally sends my body flying, but as soon as I come down from the high, I push the thought of him out of my head and start to fall asleep.

I desperately need to get laid by a regular human being.

Chapter Eight

RAFE

I didn't mean for it to go that far. I really just wanted to tease her a little bit, but her high-pitched whine in my ear made me forget this was just a game.

Then my fingertips found those bare tits, and it was over.

I can't remember the last time a woman made me feel so out of control. Thank fuck I was able to pump the brakes when I did. She kept asking me to take her into her apartment, and for a moment, I considered it.

Instead, I locked my door and did about a hundred pushups until three o'clock this morning. I don't have to be at the station until nine, so it gave me a couple hours to sleep.

I thought I could at least enjoy a cup of coffee in peace, until I hear a knock on my door around 7:30. Letting out an exhausted sigh, I pull the door open and find her standing there, freshly showered with her long auburn curls clipped back so they fall straight down her back. She's in her pastel blue scrubs, which hug her tits in a way that I've never noticed before, but now I can't seem to take my eyes off of them. I wonder if she's at least wearing a bra today.

"Good morning," I growl, coffee cup in hand.

She looks like she's preparing herself for a fight, shoulders squared, jaw set. I want to ask her if she ever made good on her promise to 'take care of herself' last night. The thought of it has the blood coursing to places other than my brain.

"I am not going to fuck you," she blurts out, and my eyes go wide.

Somewhere down the hall, a door opens and feet shuffle toward the elevator. Shelby's eyes dart away as she notices that we have an audience too. I pull her in by the strap of her shoulder bag and shut the door behind her. I don't need my neighbors thinking I'm preying on young single women in the building.

"A little early for that, isn't it?" I ask, glaring down at her. Her round doe eyes stare up at me, and I almost get lost in those wild green irises.

"This thing between us," she says, pointing back

and forth between us. "This isn't happening. That stuff you did last night was straight up manipulative."

"Manipulative?" I ask with a crooked brow. "I didn't hear you complaining."

"Well, you caught me at a weak moment. I thought I knew you, Rafe Nolan, but now I know you're just a self-centered, grumpy, manipulative asshole, and we're not having sex..."

Dropping my coffee cup on the counter, I step toward her because there's something about the way she's running her mouth at me that has me feeling like she wants this too. I never properly kissed her last night, and while she's right...this thing between us is not happening...I still can't help but think we could have a little fun with this electric hate we've created.

Before she can finish her sentence, I snatch her up by the back of the neck and pull her in for a kiss. It shuts her right up. She moans into my mouth as I taste the sweet minty flavor of her toothpaste. Her lips are soft, and I like the way her mouth relaxes against mine so I can run my tongue along the sharp edges of her teeth.

She groans as I push her body back against the wall.

"No," she whines, and I pull away. Her lips are already red where my two-day stubble has chafed them. I can tell by the look of surrender in her eyes that she doesn't want me to stop, but she said no...so I wait.

The ball's in your court now, sweetheart.

"We're not doing this," she breathes just before jumping off the wall and latching onto my face like it can save her life. As her lips attack mine this time, I gently peel her hands off my neck and face and push them behind her back. She doesn't fight it, and she almost puts them there like she wants to.

I continue to kiss her, and I love the way her movements change once her wrists are in my hands. She opens herself to me, pressing her hips forward so I can run my hand along the back of her thigh and pull her leg open like I did last night.

"We're not doing this?" I ask.

"Fuck you," she growls, letting her head hang back. "It's just sex."

The blood being pumped from my heart feels like ice when she says that. I have news for her. We are not doing this, and I'm not fucking her even though she's staring at me with those fuck me now eyes.

"I have to get to work," I whisper, leaning down to admire the marks on her neck where I nibbled on her last night. I want to leave more, and I want to leave them everywhere.

She lets out another whine as I pull away.

"Fine," she argues. Taking her arms from their spot behind her, she reaches for me, and I almost miss it. Her fingers graze the buttons of my shirt, and I snatch up her wrists with a little too much intensity.

"What the fuck?" she cries, and I quickly let them go and turn away.

"What's with you and touching?" she asks.

I don't answer her as she follows me around my apartment, watching me gather up my things.

"You can touch me, but I can't touch you?" she asks.

"I like to be in control," I answer, turning toward her to see her standing in the doorway of my bedroom. Her eyes land on the workout equipment in the corner and my bed, unmade in the middle. "I thought you liked it?" I ask.

I see her swallow, trying to hide her expression. Stepping up to her, my face just inches from hers, I whisper, "You like it, don't you? Imagine being tied up on my bed, letting me do whatever I want to you, knowing you'll love every fucking minute of it."

"We're not..." she mutters, but she doesn't finish her sentence.

"Fine," I answer, pushing past her toward the door. Holding it open for her, I say, "I get off work at 7...if you change your mind."

With one last glance at my bed, she walks straight out of my apartment, and I let her leave alone. I could leave too, but I don't think I can handle being on an elevator alone with her at the moment.

SHELBY

I spend the rest of my day feeling entirely out of alignment. Which is dangerous for a nurse. I lost count about six times today while taking heart rates, and I almost wrote down the wrong patient's name on a prescription form.

This thing needs to get settled, and by lunchtime, I have myself convinced that I will avoid Rafe at all costs. I can ignore him. I'll join a dating app and maybe meet someone new. Someone normal—with low toxicity levels.

Sure, they probably won't be into that hands-behind-my-back, tied up stuff, but there's nothing wrong with a little good old vanilla sex. Plus, I'm twenty-eight. I don't need to be worrying about getting laid right now. I need to find someone serious and focus on trying to settle down.

But then I think about that kiss. God, that kiss.

I end up eating my lunch in my car on the drive between clients. After picking up my sandwich from the drive-through, my bluetooth starts ringing in the car.

For a short split second, I actually imagine it's Rafe. I don't know why. He's never called me before. I don't even think he has my number.

Then I peer down and see Ezra's name on the screen. Clicking the button on the steering wheel, I greet him, pulling into a parking spot so I can at least scarf down my meal without the risk of driving off the road.

"Hey, Ez," I call out, but he doesn't greet me back. I just hear heavy breathing, and my heart drops. "Ezra?"

"I'm a terrible brother," he groans.

"No, you're not. Stop it."

"I am. I never should have asked you what I did. That was so fucked up. What if he finds out and takes it out on you? I should never ask you to lie for me like that."

There's so much stress in his voice, I know this probably kept him up all night. This is what Ezra does. He finds one thing to worry about, and he lets it devour him.

"I haven't done anything, Ezra. If you don't want me to do anything, I won't. Don't worry about what you asked me. I'm a big girl, you know."

"I'm such a piece of shit," he mutters.

"You are not a piece of shit," I reply. "Look, why don't we do dinner tonight?" I could use the distraction anyway.

"Yeah, that sounds good," he answers. "Can we do a late dinner? I have work stuff until seven."

My face falls. "What kind of work stuff?"

"Just work, Shelby. Stop acting like my mom."

It's always hot and cold with him. One moment, he's apologizing, the next he's snapping.

"Okay, fine. Want to meet at the Mexican place at

eight, then?"

"Sounds good," he answers, and I hear the change in his tone. He sounds pretty over the guilt and he's moving on to something else.

"Hey, Ez, don't worry about it anymore, okay?" I ask.

"Okay, but just be careful with him. If you decide to talk to him. He's fucking crazy."

You have no idea, I think but don't dare say it.

Dinner with my brother has me feeling relieved. I have an excuse to avoid Rafe's apartment. Maybe a couple days to cool off will get him out of my head. Maybe as long as I don't see him, I can stay away.

Chapter Nine

RAFE

The weekend flies by, and I don't see Shelby once. Saturday night was frustrating, to say the least. Especially after that kiss in the morning. I couldn't get the sweet taste of her lips off my mind all day. I actually had myself convinced that I could let myself go with this girl. Just so I could kiss her again.

But she doesn't show up Saturday night. Or Sunday. Her car is gone Monday morning before I leave for work, and I keep waiting for my head to just move on. She clearly has.

Work is quiet today. Mostly paperwork from the weekend, and I do my best to stay on top of the buillshit, but I need something else to keep my attention.

Opening the file on the kid arrested last week, I decide today would be a good day to do a little poking around. So I grab my jacket and head into town.

The owners of the gift shop downtown see me coming as I park the bike and walk up to the storefront. I can see when someone has something to hide before they even open their mouths to speak. It's all in how they react to seeing me. It's a different brand of fear. Fear of getting caught, and fear of causing trouble.

These people, a young couple from Juarez, have the latter written all over their faces. It was the woman's nephew who was picked up last week, and by the look she's giving me, she's currently saying about a hundred Hail Mary's in her head that I'm not here to pick him up again.

"Good morning," they both chime as I walk in the door.

"Morning," I answer, politely. "Is Mateo around?"

"He hasn't gotten into any more trouble, has he?" the girl asks, stepping toward me from behind the counter. I try to show her a reassuring smile, but it doesn't seem to be calming her down.

"Not at all. Just checking in on him," I answer, which is true. Last week, Mateo didn't drop a word to the investigators on where the drugs came from or who set him up to sell on Wicked. He just claimed he sold them because he wanted to. Got them from a kid whose name he didn't know. Typical cover-up story.

And since he's here on a visa, getting tied up in a felony could cause major problems for him and his family.

My job isn't to fuck up his life. My job is to find out whose life needs to be fucked up.

Which is exactly why I'm here.

"He's in the stockroom," the husband says. He keeps a stern expression while he stands next to his wife. I appreciate his tenacity.

Giving them both a head nod, I walk toward the back of the store. As promised, Mateo is there, unboxing a case of ceramic mugs and putting little price labels on the bottom. He doesn't hear me come in because his bluetooth headphones are so loud, I can hear Machine Gun Kelly shouting in his ear.

I tap him on the shoulder, and he nearly jumps out of his skin when he turns and sees me standing there.

Putting my hands up, I give him a small grin before pulling those earbuds out of his ears. "You know, if your aunt was up there getting robbed, you wouldn't be much help."

He spins and looks toward the front, then back at me. "I'm sorry."

I laugh. "Calm down, kid. You're not in trouble. How are you holding up?"

He shrugs. Mateo is the kind of kid who tries to look tougher than he is, not because he wants to but because he has to. It's a constant defense mechanism put in place to keep people a little afraid of how bad you could crack under pressure. Deep down, he's a decent kid, put in a shitty situation, with little to no options.

I get it because I was this exact kid. Cornered, terrified, and desperate.

Everything is out of your control, so you control what you can. That's what Mateo is doing now. He's only sixteen, and I've seen his record. He's got almost straight As at his school, and when I called around, his teachers raved about him. He doesn't deal drugs on the street because he's a criminal. He did it because it was his only choice.

And I'd rather spend every day of my job figuring out who put him in that spot before I arrest him again.

"I'm not going to ask you any more questions," I say, then glance up at him. "Unless you have anything you want to say."

He shakes his head.

"Fine. I'm stopping in to remind you that if you want to say something, I can keep you and your family safe. I've taken down other dealers in Wicked and I kept the girl who spoke up safe."

Mateo nods at me, I try to relax, sitting on a box next to him. "You came all the way down here to tell me that?" he says.

"Yeah, that and I'm just really bored at work."

He laughs. I pick up a mug from the shelf he's loading them on, and I laugh.

Let's get Wicked. One of the less gimmicky styles,

it's printed in black typeface on a white mug. I like it, and even I see the irony in that.

As I place it on the shelf in front of me, a name on the shipping label catches my eye.

Ezra Hawthorne.

Hawthorne Wholesale.

You've got to be fucking kidding me.

Grabbing the box, I look at Mateo. "Do you know this guy?"

"Ezra? Yeah he's the new manager. That's why we have all this new merch."

"I thought your aunt and uncle owned the store," I shot back a little too eager for information.

"Nah," he answered easily. "Ezra bought it after the hurricane last year. We almost lost everything."

I nearly forgot about the big storm that ripped through the coast last September. It's not out of the ordinary for Wicked to get storms, but this one hit us harder than we expected it to. A lot of businesses nearly went under after that.

And if it were anyone else who saved Mateo's family from going hungry, I would call them a hero, but this was Ezra. He never missed an opportunity to cash in where he could, and if he bought the store...using it as a front to distribute...I wouldn't be the least bit surprised.

I don't want to come on too strong at first, but pieces are suddenly coming together. If Mateo is being pressured by someone to push product around town...

someone who has something to hold over him…like his visa, this could make my job a lot easier.

"He's a good guy?" I ask, just trying to get a feel for the boy's thoughts.

He shrugs and gives me a non-committal answers. "Sure."

I knew Ezra was in town, working in distribution, but this tie between him and the recent drugs bust has to be more than a coincidence.

I have to be careful about how I approach this now. Putting too much heat on Mateo could backfire, and he'll turn to Ezra for help. The whole operation could implode before I even have a chance to make a move. But lucky for me, I have someone else I can pressure about this.

SHELBY

I make it three days before cracking. Every time I pass his door, I wonder if he's inside. I think about the way his rough lips felt against mine. My wrists in his hands.

But it was the crummy day I had today that has me standing in front of his door now. Every visit felt like bad news after bad news, and it wears me down. I need something to take my mind off of it. Something to think about other than Mrs. Yan's face when I told her to stay by her husband as much as possible because his days are almost over. Something to take my mind off the fact that he didn't smile one time to me today. Something to take my mind off the fact that I think my brother is involved in something crooked and I can't do anything to stop it.

So I wait in my apartment until I hear him enter his. Now I'm standing here, ready to knock without knowing exactly what I'm getting myself into. It could be wonderful, but it could be terrible. I could get hurt, in more ways than one.

But no matter how I look at it, I know at this moment, I don't have a choice anymore. I'm here for a reason, and I couldn't turn around if I tried. Strangely, it's not my brother's request that has me standing here, even though that's what it should be. No, there's something more intense pulling me in.

I knock three times, slowly so he knows it's me.

It's quiet a moment before I hear his voice. "Come in." It's not a warm offer, more like a command. And I obey.

His apartment is dim. The setting sun in the window behind him is all that illuminates the great room, casting him in a silhouette in front of the window. I can see the scowl on his face. He's still in his work clothes, which almost always seems to be a black button-up shirt, tight and rolled to the elbows over a pair of dark jeans.

He begins to remove his gun holster, and my mouth goes dry. "Took you long enough."

"I don't know why I'm here," I answer, still standing by the door. There's a part of my brain that realizes I haven't moved because he hasn't told me to. I retreat quickly to that thought because it separates me from every other fucked up thought I've had today.

"I do," he answers as he moves toward the kitchen. "Want a drink?"

"Yes, please," I croak. Without a word, he opens a bottle of red wine from his counter and pours a glass for each of us. Then he stalks toward me, handing me mine and never taking his eyes off of my face. For some reason, all I can think about is his bed that I know is just in the room to the right. The words of the bartender come back to me about Rafe waging wars in his bedroom, and I start to wonder if he hides ropes and whips under the mattress. What exactly did she mean by that? Is he just into rough sex and why the fuck didn't I think about this before this moment?

I certainly do not trust him enough for this, and I feel like an idiot for even coming over. Panic settles in as my eyes roam his sculpted shoulders hiding under that shirt. He's a lot bigger than me and definitely a lot stronger than me. Every rational thought in my head is screaming at me to get out of there, but the part of my brain being run by my body, which desperately needs to be fucked, is telling me to stay.

My brain wins out.

"I shouldn't have come here," I stammer, dropping the wine on the counter and turning toward the door. I only get about three steps when his booming voice behind me stops me in my tracks.

"Stop"

Facing the door, I feel his presence behind me. He steps so close, his body brushes mine, and I wait, my breath stuck in my throat. When his lips finally meet the back of my neck, I let out a shudder. Soft lips trails over my shoulder until his rough hand is twisting my head so his mouth can meet mine.

"Hands on the door," he mumbles against my lips. It's obvious that he needs to be in control. He's constantly telling me what to do with my hands. He won't let me touch him, but he can touch me.

"Is this a power thing for you?" I ask, letting out a gasp as his hand snakes its way around my body and up my shirt again. I still haven't followed his instructions of putting my hands on the door, but it hasn't slowed down his lips. So I keep them clutched at my sides.

He doesn't answer me.

"Are you into that kind of stuff? BDSM? I just think I should know—" His hands cut off my words as he plunges them down the front of my pants and grips my sex in his coarse hands.

"Hands on the door" he growls again, this time firmer. He rubs my clit roughly, and my hands fly to the door. The pressure from his touch is enough to start a fire in my body. Beneath the pleasure, there's a hint of pain that only fans the flames. It's been so long since I have been touched by anyone down there,

I can't stop the way my hips buck, trying to coax his fingers to keep moving.

"Into what?" he asks as he plays between my legs.

I can barely form a sentence. "It's okay if you are, I just—I think I should...ahh," I cry out as he hoists me away from the door and tosses me over his shoulder. This is the part where he takes me to his bedroom, and I literally have no idea what's around the corner. Ezra told me to be careful with him, and this is the opposite of careful. The fear doesn't cool off the heat in my body...it accelerates it.

But to my shock, he drops me on the couch, and doesn't pause before moving for the hem of my shirt to pull it over my head. Once I'm sitting in my bra, feeling completely blindsided, he starts to tear my pants down.

I came here for hate sex. I won't lie to myself about that. There's a certain level of intimacy I want tonight, which is none at all. Which is why I cannot understand why I reach up and pull his mouth in for a kiss. Kissing is not a part of hate sex.

When my hands touch his cheeks, he yanks his body away.

For a torturously long moment, he stares at me, but I already know what he's about to say. I could argue with him about the touching stuff or I could get exactly what I came here to get. So before he can utter a word, I put my hands behind my back, shoved between my body at the couch, and when he sees that

I'm behaving, he leans in and devours my mouth with his.

As soon as his lips touch mine I remember why I wanted it. Rafe's kisses are aggressive, yet quiet. When our mouths are joined, I don't feel his hatred anymore. It's the only time I don't feel his hatred, and it's in that silent, intimate connection that my belly pools with heat.

Before I know it, his hands are in the waistband of my scrubs again, and they come off in one eager swoop. Now, I'm sitting completely naked on his couch while he's still fully dressed. But I can't move to take off his clothes because my hands are stuck behind me.

I hardly have time to notice as his mouth travels down my neck, straight down the center of my chest to my belly where he takes a slight nibble.

I'm completely breathless when his hand finds the gentle folds between my legs. Then his mouth his there, his lips around my sex, and his tongue devouring me like he's starving.

I feel his eyes on my face as I writhe on the couch, a little self-conscious of how not-long I'm going to last. I haven't had a man down there in a long time—fuck, maybe a year. And Rafe is not holding back at all. When his two fingers sink deep, I yelp, almost moving my hands to grip his hair more than once.

Just as I feel my climax closing in, he pulls away. Waiting for him to climb up here and fuck me right, I finally open my eyes and peer down at him. He has a wicked smile as he dives back in.

Two more times, he stops just when I'm about to reach the pinnacle.

"Rafe, please," I beg when he halts his movements again.

"Please what?" he teases.

"Stop torturing me," I cry, my back arching off the couch as he hooks his fingers and hits the spot that makes me see stars.

Suddenly, my legs are clenched around him and I'm flying. His hands are all over my body. His lips and his tongue own me.

As my body relaxes against the couch, he stands, towering over me with a wicked look on his face. Eager to reach for him, I pull my hands out and put my hand out toward him. He doesn't take it.

"Feel better?" he asks as he walks away.

"What?"

"I can tell you've been on edge. Did you get that out of your system?" He reaches his wine glass, and suddenly I feel extremely exposed, naked on his couch. In a scramble, I reach for my clothes and throw them on, feeling like a bigger fool than ever.

"Wait. That's it?" I ask, following him to the bathroom.

"Unsatisfied?" he asks with a snarky tone.

"I just thought we would..."

"What? Fuck? I distinctly remember you standing at my door and telling me very adamantly that we would not be doing exactly that."

I stand there, mouth hanging open as he brushes past me with a duffel bag in his hands. "Is this all a game to you?"

But he doesn't answer. Instead, he leaves through the front door of his apartment like nothing happened.

Chapter Ten

RAFE

My body feels like a cinder block of fucking tension at the moment. And laying into this punching bag really isn't helping as much as it normally does. I can still taste her on my lips.

I almost broke. It was too close.

Fuck that.

I couldn't get out of that apartment fast enough.

My shirt is now sweat-soaked, so I tear it off and throw it in the corner. The basement is still dark except for the red light in the corner. I'm sure she's back in her place by now, but I'm not ready to go upstairs yet. There's still a raging hard-on in my pants, and it's uncomfortable as fuck.

What would have happened if I took her to my bedroom instead of the couch? Would I have caved? Finally given in. Finally taken back my life and sent a big fuck-you to the assholes who messed me up so bad as a kid that I can't get off as an adult.

I would have fallen to fucking pieces right in front of her afterward. No thank you.

I'm stronger than these urges. Just to prove it, I slam my fist into the punching bag over and over. Punching out the reminder that I'm a sick fuck.

It must be nice to be like Murph or Logan. They have no shame, not like me. I can only assume getting into bed with their girls wasn't such a mind fuck. And the only person who ever knew my secrets is dead now, and I buried it with Theo, but I still have to deal with this shit every day.

He was the one who told me to start fighting. That I had so much pent up aggression, and I always seemed to be expressing it poorly so we went to Vic's together.

Now Theo's gone, but my issues haven't gone anywhere.

Lucky fucking me.

There's a scuff against the floor, and I spin, ready to throw a punch when I see Shelby creeping through the darkness, watching me with wide eyes. She puts her hands up as her gaze travels across my bare chest and the pitched tent in my pants. Turning my body, I hide it with my back to her.

"Go home," I bark, but this time she doesn't listen.

"Will you just talk to me for a minute?" she whispers through the darkness.

"I'm not a big talker," I grunt, taking another shot at the bag.

She's closer now, and I clench my jaw as she casts a shadow from the red light behind her. I wish she'd just go home. Her presence is only making things worse.

"Is that how you always are with women? Just do that...and leave?" she asks.

"Never heard a complaint before."

"Rafe," she says, and I send her a glance before turning away and sticking to my one-two cadence. She doesn't want to get into this right now. I know she doesn't, but if she doesn't stop pushing me, I'm going to fucking explode on her.

Just when I'm about to yell at her again, I feel the warm skin of her hands against my back, and every muscle in my body tenses. Acting on instinct, I spin ready to throw fists, but thankfully, she's too close, and I gather her body up in my arms instead. She lets out a scream as her back slams against the wall, and I snatch one of her wrists in each of my hands.

My breath is heavy only inches away from her face, but she doesn't cower away. Her head rests to the side of my shoulder, giving me full access to bury my face into her neck.

After a long moment of heavy breathing and silence, she whispers, "I'm sorry."

"Don't do that again," I mumble, squeezing her wrists above her head.

"I won't."

Softly, I feel her hips grind toward me, rubbing a delicious friction against the stiffness pressed against her body. For once, I actually let her move against me until we're moving together, and I tilt my hips in tandem with hers.

"Why are you torturing yourself?" she asks, opening her legs for me.

My movement stops. Moving away from her, I try not to let her words sink in. This isn't torture. I refuse to call it that. This isn't torture.

"Let me help you," she murmurs, pressing her body toward me. Before she can reach me, I pull away and grab my bag from its place near the door.

"I don't need your help."

Quickly, I disappear through the door and rush up the stairs to my apartment.

SHELBY

I can't sleep. Whenever I close my eyes, I see the snarl on his face after my fingers drifted across the cool, moist skin of his back.

Every few minutes, I convince myself that it's nothing. I'm looking into too much, and I need to drop it. Rafe is nothing but a miserable jerk who likes to use sex as a tool of manipulation. What he did to me on the couch was amazing...but there was nothing emotional tied to it for him. He was just trying to get me off his back.

But I've sure as fuck never been with a guy who just wanted to get me off and get nothing in return. Rafe wouldn't even let me touch him.

I toss again, unable to quiet my mind enough to sleep.

He snapped when I touched his back. It was instinct, and he's never let me touch him. He's always kept my hands back when we kissed. Does he never let anyone touch him? Ever?

But if no one can touch him...then how does he have sex with them? Does he really make the women he sleeps with keep their hands restrained the entire time?

Unless he doesn't have sex at all...

I flip again in my bed. This is ridiculous. Why do I even care? So he's fucked up and has some serious issues. He doesn't give two shits about me, so why should I care about him?

Then I replay the moments on the couch ten years ago. I kissed him, touched his face, and for a moment, he let me. Just before he pushed me away and never spoke to me again. From that moment, he hated me.

Did Rafe really have so many emotional scars that he has always been this haunted?

What exactly happened to him as a kid that he behaves this way? I know he spent some time in and out of foster care, but he certainly never talked about that much in high school. Probably not much of a chance I could get him to open up about it now.

It's none of my business.

I repeat those words over and over to myself, trying to get myself to sleep, but it's not working. Finally, the sky turns a light shade of pink and orange, and I climb out of bed. I give up.

It's my day off anyway.

For a moment, while drinking my coffee and trying to pretend I got any rest at all, I convince myself that I'm not going to think about Rafe today. But I don't get far. Because on my second cup, I remember my best friend from nursing school, Jillian, who works at the health department and was always a fan of a little rule bending.

As I pull up my phone to text her, I pause. I can't seriously be thinking of this. I could lose my licence to practice. I could lose everything. It's a stupid, stupid risk.

But I have to know.

Jillian is off today too, so after a quick catch-up session, she agrees to come out to Wicked today to meet for coffee and help me with whatever devious things I'm up to (her words). As I sit at the coffee shop on the boardwalk, I keep second guessing this plan. It's a major invasion of privacy, not to mention incredibly illegal.

There's a new coffee shop attached to the locally owned bookstore on the main drag where Jillian finds me taking up a small table in the back with my cappuccino. She throws her arms around me before sitting across from me.

"I can't believe you moved to the beach!" she squeals. "I'm so jealous."

"I love it."

Immediately she digs into my love life, because Jillian is nothing if not a major gossip queen. Which is just another reason why I know she will help me. After some small talk and catch up conversations about her new fiance and my life living as a hospice nurse, she finally starts digging into what I need to know.

"Okay, so tell me whose file I need to find for you," she smiles with a cup up to her lips.

Except for an older couple reading in the corner, it's just us and the young woman who's working in the aisles of the store. I look around nervously before I talk discreetly over the table.

"It's an old friend from high school. He was in foster care as a kid, and I know there are files with CPS."

"A new boyfriend with some emotional baggage?" she asks.

"I'm worried about him. He's...struggling, and I

just want to help him." This much is true, more so than I even realized until now.

"Well it might take me some time, but I can probably dig it up for you. They don't keep those things forever, though. Just a heads up."

My stomach turns. This is wrong.

"I feel awful for even asking."

"Don't. Your intentions are good. Plus there's like no oversight on these things anymore, so you don't have to worry about getting in trouble. They have their hands full with plenty of other stuff."

"Well, if it makes any better, he's a cop," I say, rolling my eyes and finishing my coffee.

I feel eyes on us from across the store, and I turn to see the young, blonde bookstore employee watching us carefully. I turn back to Jillian to make small talk, hoping she didn't just hear what we were talking about.

Jillian and I sit there for another hour before she finally stands to hug me and promises to send me everything she can, and I'm already a ball of nerves just thinking about it.

After she walks out, I sit back at the table and drop my face into my hands. I'll text her later and tell her to forget about it. She won't go back to work until tomorrow anyway, so I have time to back out. It's not worth being suspended.

But how can I help him if I don't understand what is wrong with him? And why the hell am I trying to help him anyway? Wasn't I just trying to spy on him for Ezra so I could help make his life hell? Don't I hate him?

Just then a pair of small white Chucks fills my vision under the table.

"I'm sorry to pry," the pretty blonde says as she takes the seat opposite me. There are a few other people in the small cafe now, but she keeps her voice down as she stares at me.

"Hi," I mumble, waiting for her to say she's going to report me for breaking HIPAA violations.

"You said something, and I didn't mean to eavesdrop, but I think the person you're talking about is a friend of mine."

Oh Jesus, Mary, and Joseph.

"I'm sorry, I'm not actually planning on doing any-thing—" I stammer.

"I can tell you exactly what is in that file. If it even still exists."

I fall silent, staring at her with questions flying around my head. "I don't understand."

"You're talking about Rafe Nolan, aren't you?" she whispers.

I nod.

"Would you like to go for a walk?" she asks.

It's not so much a walk as her taking me to a quieter part of the boardwalk where she can stare at me skeptically. She tells me her name is Sierra, and I can tell by the way she keeps glancing back at the shop that she's nervous about talking to me.

"I heard you talking to your friend, and I just have to say something."

"Listen, I don't know what you heard, but I'm a nurse, and I was just—"

"It's fine," she says, interrupting me. "I understand. He's...mysterious."

"You think?" I blurt out with a laugh, and she smiles back at me.

"Can I ask? Are you two...?"

I bite my lip. Are we what, together? How do I answer this? I decide to go with the truth, or at least as much of it as I can part with. "Rafe and I knew each other a long time ago. We were friends in high school, until things went south. I'm trying to make things right with him, but I'm afraid he won't even let me in enough to do that."

She nods, like she knows exactly what I'm talking about.

"Well, I won't tell you what I know, because those are his secrets to tell, but I can at least give you some warning." We start walking away from the shop as we talk. "Rafe was in foster care as a kid. He didn't have it easy—well, none of them did, but Rafe especially suffered, and I think he's going to carry that with him for the rest of his life."

"Did he tell you this?" I ask. The girl looks too bright-eyed and bushy-tailed to be any ex or friend of

Rafe's, but I'm almost a little jealous that she knows more than me.

"No. Rafe confided a lot in my boyfriend's brother, who passed the information on before he died. Rafe is not going to just come out and say it."

"I assumed that much," I answer.

She's quiet a moment before she says, "I don't know what your intentions are, but I hope you can help him. I want him to be happy."

"I do want to help him," I say.

"Rafe is like family to us," she adds, and I wince at the statement. He called me his family once, and I walked away from him for a long time. Getting him to open up to me is going to be nearly impossible now.

As I walk back to my apartment, I shoot a text to Jillian, telling her thanks for coffee, but I don't need those records after all. I don't know what changed since, and I don't feel like I know anything more than I did earlier, but maybe it's just the new knowledge that I'm not the only person on Wickett who cares about him, and I don't even know when that happened.

It's like I forgot that I hated him. I was supposed to be sabotaging him, but now all I can think about is getting to a place where he'll let me place my palms on his skin. And maybe he never will, and maybe I'll still end up hating him when this is all over, but the only thing I do know for sure now is that I cannot hurt him anymore than he's already been hurt.

But there just might be a way to help him.

Chapter Eleven

RAFE

Mondays are the worst. It's like the whole goddamn beach goes nuts over the weekend and leaves me a mess to clean up when I get back to the office. There's a stack of paperwork on my desk that I barely make a dent in by the time I head home after eight.

All I want to do when I get home is crack open the bottle and spend a few rounds in the basement. A trip to Vic's would be nice, but I don't have the energy tonight.

I haven't seen Shelby since our little rendezvous over the weekend. She disappeared for most of the day Sunday, which is for the best. Things got a little too close with her in my apartment.

What she and I need now is distance. As much of it as we can get.

But as I get off the elevator on my floor, I sense a change in the air right away. I freeze in front of my door when I notice something hanging from the door-knob. It's a soft, black rope about two feet long. It's tied gently in a knot and hangs on my door without anything else. Not a note or a warning.

I know it's from her immediately.

Why she left it is a mystery.

Is she trying to seduce me? Or is this a joke to her?

Without thinking, I grab the rope from the door and open my apartment, almost nervous that she'll be there waiting like some sort of crazy fucking stalker, but my apartment is empty. I toss my keys and phone on the counter and stare at the rope in my hands.

It's soft, and there's just enough there to bind something together, like wrists or ankles. It's not enough to tie someone to a bed rail or anything.

Before I can think about it anymore, I toss it on the dining room table and move toward the bottle of bourbon waiting on the counter. The first glass goes down easily.

I'm just pouring my second when there's a gentle knock on the door.

Here we fucking go.

"Come in," I bark, and I wait as she steps into my

still-dim space. I only turned on the one small light by the door when I came in, so I'm bathed in darkness by the kitchen.

"What the fuck is this?" I ask, pointing to the item she left on my door.

"I did my research," she says, stepping toward me. There's something different about her today. She's walking with more confidence, and it's sexy as fuck.

"What research was that?" I ask, taking another drink.

"Some people are turned on by having control, and others are turned on by giving the control to others."

Jesus. She thinks I'm into this bondage stuff. I roll my eyes with a groan. "I'm no dom, Shelby. That's not—"

"I know you're not," she whispers, not backing down. As she takes another step, her face eases into the dim light from the moon, and I nearly lose my breath. She's wearing makeup, or at least more than usual. Her hair is held back at the nape of her neck, and the look on her face says she's being serious as a fucking heart attack.

"I have a suspicion about you, Rafe, and I don't expect you to admit or not, because this thing you're holding back from isn't because you want to."

My eyes narrow at her, and I have to wet my lips because of my mouth going dry. Then, my eyes travel downward, and I notice she's in nothing more than a silk dress that comes just low enough to cover the apex of her thighs.

The perfection of her appearance feeds a hate deep within me. She's so fucking beautiful it makes me angry. And not only on the outside, but her soul is so goddamn pure that I can't even look at her. She's coming here to help me, like she constantly does, and it doesn't make sense. It's just easier to despise her for it than accept that I deserve it.

"You think me tying you up is going to help me?" I ask. She's close now, within reach.

"I think if you know I can't touch you, you'll let yourself go."

"How do you know what I need?" I breathe as her body stops just inches away from me.

Turning her eyes down, she whispers. "I just do."

I can't take it another second, so I yank her body against mine by the back of her neck. Crashing my mouth against hers, I notice the way she holds her hands behind her without me even having to ask.

My hands roam the landscape of her body, drifting down to her ass which is barely hiding under this silk nightie. My hands squeeze the bare flesh as I press her against the wall of my kitchen. She moans into my lips.

"Tie me up," she gasps, and I pull away, looking toward the table where I dropped the rope.

She's panting now as I return, ready to bind it around her wrists. Suddenly, I stop. This seems crazy.

What the fuck is wrong with me? I'm not one of those freaks who needs something bizarre to get him off. I shouldn't be doing this to her just because I need it.

Her parted lips wait for me, and my head feels full of fog. I can't think straight. Why am I doing this? What good could possibly come from this? I can't be her boyfriend. She can't heal me. No matter what she tries, it will never change what I am, and when she figures that out, she'll regret every second of this.

Not to mention...I'm supposed to be asking her about Ezra. That's what I really need. Not trying to figure out a way to get off.

I press the rope into her hands. "Go home, Shelby."

"But—" she protests, but I don't give her a chance to fight me. I walk to the door and open it, waiting for her to leave. This isn't an expression of dislike. In fact, it's quite the opposite. I'm doing the same thing I did ten years ago, giving her an opportunity to avoid something she'd regret.

She stares at me in shock for a moment, and guilt washes over me when I take another glance at her silk dress. She went through a lot of trouble to do this for me, but I'm too fucked up to give her what she wants.

Finally, after a moment, she stomps out the door just before tossing the rope to the floor without so much as a glance in my direction.

SHELBY

I'm such an idiot.

I just put my own head in the guillotine and for some reason act surprised when the blade came down. I must be really horny.

What was I thinking? That if I seduced him enough he would give in and all of the trauma the blonde girl clued me in on would just go away?

And why? Why do I even care? Because the sex would be good? Because I believe deep down that two people who hate each other can screw as passionately as ones who love each other?

No. This thing between Rafe and I goes deeper than that. It's more than just fixing him because I can. The seeds were planted ten years ago, and the passion between us burns too bright to ignore. There's no point in analyzing why I am drawn to him because it doesn't change the fact that I am.

The real question is: what am I going to do about it now?

Getting into my apartment, I immediately pull off the black lingerie I pulled out from the corner of my closet this morning and throw it right back where it belongs. Lingerie is a waste. Men clearly want a woman naked or not at all.

Okay, that was too harsh, but I can't shake the bitterness that's flowing through my veins. I need something, and I need it now. Rushing to put on my jeans and a snug sweatshirt from college, I quickly order a car on my phone. I may not have any friends on Wickett, but I do have a bartender...which is the saddest thing I've ever told myself.

As I walk into Smokey's, I notice Laini right away. She's throwing darts with an old man with gray hair and a hearty laugh. He calls her darlin' when she beats him and runs back to the bar. Already, just being in this environment, I feel better. There are sports games playing on every screen along the walls, and there are more people in tonight than the last time I came.

"You came back!" Laini shouts as I walk up to the bar. For a moment, I feel a little paranoid that she's somehow figured out that I was spying a little last time I was here, but as she starts preparing my vodka soda with lime, I realize that we're still good. I didn't actually do anything wrong anyway.

As I plop down on the stool, I smile at her.

"Nurses get the first one free," she says proudly as she sets my drink in front of me.

"Nurse?" the gray haired man shouts from behind me. "The second one's on me!"

Beaming, I wave at him, and my shoulders already feel so much lighter than they did an hour ago when Rafe's lips were on me, just moments before he shut me down and humiliated me.

"How was the fight?" Laini asks, and I shake my head with confusion. "At Vic's," she adds.

"Oh," I answer, remembering the last time I was in here and how I left in a rush. "Interesting," I reply.

"I bet," she laughs. "Do you like boxing?"

"Me? No," I say with a shake of my head.

"I bet it feels good to punch someone," she adds while drying a glass. "I'd be willing to give it a try."

"As long as we can pick who we punch, right?" I add, and we laugh. My drink is going down fast. I feel the alcohol loosening my muscles as I melt into the chair.

"Hey, speaking of. How is Rafe?" she asks, giving me a look with a bite of her lip and fidget in her fingers that tells me maybe she's a little too curious about Rafe.

When I walked in the door, I decided that I did not want to talk about him here. I just wanted to be a regular adult woman who has a drink in public to relax and have fun. But of course, like everything else these days, it always comes back to him.

"He's good, I guess. I rarely see him," I lie. "He works a lot."

"To be honest," Laini adds, leaning against the bar. "I hadn't thought about him in a long time since you brought him up the other day. Really threw me for a loop, and I can't get the guy out of my head now. Are you two...?"

My skin burns hot as I stare at her. How the hell am I supposed to answer that?

"Ummm...." I drawl, staring down at my drink.

"Enough said," Laini laughs. "I remember that phase of dating Rafe Nolan all too well. And for that, you need another drink." As she turns away to start making my drink, the hearty voiced old man saddles up to the barstool next to me.

"Officer Nolan?" he asks. He looks like a kind man, with a stark white Tom Selleck mustache and copper tan skin.

"Yeah," I mumble. Seriously, why can't we stop talking about him? Does everyone have history with this guy?

"He saved my daughter's life. I owe that guy everything."

My heart stops as I stare at the guy. Rafe saved someone? Mister broody boxer with an attitude problem is capable of doing good?

"Oh yeah," Laini calls from the ice machine. "I forgot about that, Tom."

"How?" I breathe.

Laini sets down my drink as I stare at the man.

"She got mixed up with a bad crowd after high school. Got picked up for having some drugs on her. We tried to keep her home with us, but she was addicted. Didn't care what her mother and I had to say, but Rafe didn't stop. He checked up on her nearly every day. Helped us keep tabs on her. He tracked down the guys who were selling to her, and when he found her passed out in the backseat of her car, he did CPR until the ambulance came."

"Oh, my God," I gasp.

"She's been clean six years now," he says proudly, and he and Laini raise their glasses. I slowly bring mine up to meet his, trying to reconcile this version of Rafe with the one I know. I'm fairly certain that checking up on addicts after they've been released is not part of his job. Why would he do that?

After Tom and Laini take turns buying me drinks, I buy them each a round and before I know it, it's two o'clock in the morning, and Laini is walking me out to my Uber. I give her a tight hug, like she's my new best friend.

She mumbles something to me about not giving up on him, but honestly, my head is too drunk to catch it all.

When I crawl into my bed, I lie there feeling stunned and lost. I don't understand how this all happened. He hated me. I hated him. But now...my heart surges when I think of what he did for that girl and her family. And the pain he hiding underneath it all.

Quickly, I find my phone on the nightstand, and I open up my text messages, typing one out to Ezra.

I can't do this anymore. I'm sorry, but I refuse to help you cause someone pain, no matter how bad they hurt us.

I don't hit send though. I stare at the message for a while, tossing these choices back and forth in my head. This will crush Ezra. No matter what I do, one of them will feel pain because of me.

Chapter Twelve

RAFE

"You drive a motorcycle?" Mateo asks as I pull up to the shop. He's working on the display out front, and he's staring at my bike like it's the coolest thing he's ever seen.

"Yeah, why?" I ask, cutting the engine and hopping off.

He walks up to inspect it, and I can see the glimmer in his eye. "Don't get any ideas," I laugh, dropping a heavy hand on his shoulder.

"I've always wanted to ride a motorcycle."

"Yeah? Well, they're dangerous."

"You drive one," he replies, glaring up at me with a

skeptical look on his face.

"I'm not sixteen."

He throws his hands up at me and starts mumbling something at me in Spanish that makes me laugh. I like this kid, which is maybe why I keep finding myself here.

But then it could also be that I can't be in my apartment anymore, not after what happened with Shelby. I was all twisted up in my head last night after I sent her packing. Then I heard her leave shortly and stay gone until after two, and I really shouldn't give a shit what she's up to, but my anxiety had fun with that one.

Getting closer to her only reminds me that her brother is somehow tied to all of this, and now that I know he's connected to Mateo, I can't let my guard down now.

"So, anything new around here?" I ask as I walk toward the display of keychains and umbrellas.

"Not unless you want to buy a Wicked Beach hat that is also a bottle opener," he says, holding a bright pink hat out to me.

"No, thanks," I grimace, and he laughs. "You know what I'm talking about, Mateo."

The smile doesn't fade easily as he groans. "No, sir. I've been good."

"I bet you have, but you still don't remember any names?"

"No," he mumbles, looking down. I know this is

hard for him. He doesn't want to lie to a cop, but the kid has honor, and it's possible he's protecting someone. I'm not going to put him in that position if I don't have to.

"Hey, Mr. Hawthorne isn't around is he?" I ask, peeking into the store. His aunt waves hesitantly at me.

"Nah," Mateo answers. "He only comes by at the end of the day to close, but then he has to rush to his second job."

My spine snaps straight. "What second job?"

"I don't know," Mateo answers with a shrug. "He just rushes off every night, always looking at his watch."

"Really," I reply, less of a question and more of a statement. "Alright, I gotta run," I say as I turn toward the bike. The kid looks confused as he watches me leave.

"Hey, if you keep up your grades maybe I'll show you how to ride this thing."

His eyes light up like it's Christmas morning.

"Don't play with me, officer," he grins, pointing at me.

"I'm serious. You don't get in trouble and get all As by the end of the semester, it's a deal."

"A's and B's," he shouts as the engine roars.

"All A's."

He puts his hands on the top of his head with a laugh and turns back to his work. As I start to pull out of my spot, I start to hope that he's not as smart in school as his teachers made him sound.

Seeing Mateo today puts me in a good mood. He makes me laugh, and after the heavy-as-fuck night I had, I needed that. Not to mention, I have something new to look into: this secret job of Ezra's.

When I get in my apartment, I open the windows, flooding the space with light, and I walk out onto the patio, the sound of the ocean waves soothing my restless mind. Quickly, I sneak a glance at her patio, but it's empty.

When I walk back inside, I spot the black rope sitting on the floor. Maybe it's my sudden chipper mood, but I'm starting to think I was too harsh last night. She was just trying to help—by letting me tie her up no less, and I was a dickhead about it.

What if I had gone through with it? I'm not saying it would fix me, but how much worse could things get? Even if I just do what I did to her on the couch again, at least I would know I tried.

At least she'd be getting something out of it before I start hounding her about Ezra's new side hustle.

Jesus, Rafe.

I let my head fall hard against the glass of the patio door. As if I needed anymore proof that I am not cut from the same cloth as Logan and Murph. They've settled easily into the boyfriend life, committing to their women without a problem, and I'm over here forcing myself to hate Shelby because I can't risk feeling the opposite.

I wrote off the possibility of being intimate with a woman years ago. Once I realized that what those fucking monsters did to me screwed me up so bad that I would never be normal, I gave up on normal. I gave up on the idea of ever having a girlfriend, getting married, having children. I convinced myself that I could live my life devoted to my job, keeping Wicked safe. That could be enough for me, and considering I could be much worse off if I hadn't been removed from that home when I was, I see this life as a blessing.

Then, Shelby showed up. And I'm pretty sure she's figured it out. How fucked up I am, and I refuse to fucking say those words out loud. She can assume as much as she wants, but if she thinks I'm going to utter those words, "I'm a fucking virgin," she's crazy. It's not going to happen.

And yet, she still sticks around. Even when I'm an asshole. When I yell at her and push her away. She's doing something to my head that's actually making me feel like I can let go. Bu tat this point, hope isn't worth having.

So I don't know why I walk over to her apartment. Why I put the rope on her door handle. Why I knock and walk away. I know she's in there. I saw her car out front, but I don't want to face her unless she wants to face me, so I put the ball in her court. She has the rope now, and if she can forgive the way I acted last night, maybe she'll come over. Maybe we can see just how far this thing can go.

SHELBY

The rope is hanging on my door when I open it, which can mean one of two things: one, he's giving it back and doesn't want anything to do with me or my kinky ideas anymore; or two, it's an invitation.

I spent most of the day nursing this hangover. And I've only been feeling mostly human for the past hour or so, so I walk to my bathroom, eager to take a shower while I think about my next move.

Plus I kind of want to make him stew for a few minutes.

The stories I heard about him in the bar last night shed all kinds of new light on the image I had of Rafe from my own experience. Based on the evidence now, he's literally been nicer to the people he arrests than to me. That's not a great sign.

But he's also shown me something stronger than kindness. I've seen his heart. Even from high school, I was one of the few people who could see Rafe with his guard down. I saw the tenderness, the fear, the hatred. And hatred is as intimate as love.

I can't turn my back on him. Even if he does hate me.

My mind was made up the moment I opened my door to find the rope. No matter what he meant by giving it back, there's only one way to find out.

After I throw on some clothes and comb my wet hair, I walk over to his door—rope in hand. It doesn't take him long to call, "Come in," after I knock. I open it hesitantly and peek my head in without any expression on my face.

He's quiet for a moment as I step in. Sitting at the dining room table, he doesn't even look up at me. "I'm sorry for the way I acted last night."

"It's okay," I mumble, walking up to the table.

"You hungry?" he asks, and it throws me off. Hungry? We don't really do the non-sex stuff, like eating together and hanging out. But the idea immediately gives me a small thrill.

"Yes," I answer, sitting at the table opposite him. When he looks up, he aims a cold, hard stare on my face, and it's a chilling feeling, being under his gaze, but he eventually softens, his lips peeling back at the corners for a small smirk that creates tiny creases in his eyes.

I don't think I've ever seen him smile.

Then, he's up and walking to the kitchen. "You like steak?"

"Of course," I answer.

Every once in a while he glances back at me while he cooks, and I melt in his suddenly softer demeanor. He's better today, and maybe it had something to do with what happened last night. Or maybe it was something else. Or someone else.

Finally, he puts a plate in front of me, and it's nice to eat with someone like this. Almost like a date. Still he doesn't say much, but the steak is delicious, paired with steamed vegetables and rice. I have to say I'm surprised. I didn't expect Rafe to be the kind of guy who could cook.

"This is delicious. Thank you," I say, savoring the last bite of medium rare steak.

After the meal is done, we settle on the couch, and he turns on the big screen TV in his living room. I don't even own a TV, so it's nice to recline on the couch next to him.

"What do you want to watch?" he asks, scrolling through Netflix.

"I have no clue what's even out. You pick."

He groans, and I laugh. It can't be easy to pick a movie for a woman when you never have company, but he settles on the latest superhero flick, which keeps enough of my attention so that when I lie back on his couch, he lifts my legs onto his lap, rubbing up to my thigh, and I barely notice. I almost don't catch when toward the end of the movie, his hand starts to slide higher.

My belly lights up with sparks when my eyes meet his, and there's hunger in his gaze.

"We don't have to do anything," I say, and I don't know why those words come out of my mouth. I keep my hands resting above my head on the arm of the couch.

"I want to," he answers, reaching for the button of my jeans, and for a moment, I consider letting him, but I'm afraid of falling into this pattern. And it's insane of me to complain about this—a man who only wants to please me, but this doesn't help him at all. I want him to feel what I feel, and it's just not the same for me if I know he's struggling. I can still imagine the pain he was in last night.

"Rafe, wait," I stammer, putting my hands up without touching him. Quickly I sit up, since lying down seems to only invite trouble. He takes a heavy breath, looking annoyed.

"What if..." I mumble, not exactly sure how I should approach this question. "What if we tried something else?"

"Like what?" he growls, his eyebrows wrinkling a crease right in the middle of his forehead.

"I don't know. There are a lot of things we can do... things I can do...without touching you." My cheeks flush, red hot as the words come out of my mouth, and I can tell he wants to say no. But he hesitates.

"Shelby," he says with a warning. "You don't understand—"

"You don't have to tell me anything if you don't want to."

His shoulders relax, like the burden of having to explain himself was weighing him down.

"You've already made me feel good," I say, clenching my fists to keep from reaching for him. "I just want to do the same thing for you."

"I don't know if I can," he finally mutters, and I see the effort it took to just say those words. He's not the kind of guy who easily admits defeat.

"Let's try it, and if you can't do it...then we'll stop."

I wait patiently, and the restraint it takes to not jump on him is one of the hardest things I've ever done. Finally, he nods.

I move down off the couch until I'm kneeling between his legs, staring up into his dark eyes. His pulse thumps rapidly through the vein in his neck, and I let my eyes trail down his face from the stubble on his cheeks to his solid chest and down to his abs I see peeking out between his shirt and pants. I want to touch it so bad, run my fingers over the washboard and around his pecs. I forgot what it felt like to wrap my hands around a man's muscled shoulders and feel a bare chest pressed up against mine. My mouth waters just thinking about it.

Slowly, my hands reach for the zipper of his pants, and on instinct, his fingers wrap around my wrist with a fierce squeeze. Our eyes locked, I let him hold my arms as I continue unbuttoning his pants.

My heart wants to crack my ribcage in half with as fast as its beating in my chest. Every second feels like torture as I pull open his jeans and peel down his boxers, my fingers brushing the soft skin of his abdomen.

Then, my mouth goes dry as I see the thick hardness that springs forth.

His chest is moving so fast with his breath, and my wrists are still held tightly in his hands. I keep my eyes on his face when I move forward, placing a wet kiss on the soft, pink head. His hips jerk as soon as I make contact, and I watch his face morph into anguish.

"Are you okay?" I whisper.

"Get the rope," he answers in a strangled gasp.

Following his request, I retrieve the black satin from my back pocket and hold it in my hands, presenting it to him like a sacrifice. I see a click in his jaw as he stares at it, contemplating his next move.

"Why are you doing this for me?" he asks.

"Have you considered that maybe I want this too?"

Leaning down, he runs his tongue over my lips, and I smile. Then, he quickly binds my wrists together. It's tight enough to keep me from pulling them apart, but not uncomfortable.

Something in his demeanor changes the moment my hands are restrained. It gives him freedom, and the confident shift in his attitude sends a warm shock to my core.

His lips find mine again, and this kiss is hungrier as he takes a sharp bite of my lips.

As he reclines back, he watches me come forward again, this time trailing my tongue along the length of his cock. The groan that escapes sounds involuntary, and I can't tell if I'm hurting him or making him feel good, but I do it again, two more times just to watch how he reacts. His head falls back on the couch, his eyes closed tightly. His hips twist like he's fighting the urge to run.

Finally, I encircle my lips around him, letting him glide over my tongue to the back of my throat. I expect him to react harshly again, but something in him melts. His hand digs into my hair, holding my head in a power move that makes me whimper. Slowly, I move up and down on his length, keeping my eyes on him for any sign that it's too much.

Especially when I feel him tighten back up, his breath growing more panicked, and I know he's close. I don't want to stop, but I can tell he wants to bolt again.

Honestly I have no idea how he did this to me without any release of his own afterwards. I'm so turned on that I know one touch to myself would send me flying.

"Shelby," he gasps and I release him, looking at his face. I want to drown in his tortured eyes while he fights against this thing his body wants so bad. I want him to have it more than anything.

"It's okay," I whisper, and he finally relaxes again so I can take him back between my lips. His fingers dig into my hair as he fucks my mouth. This time when he gets wound so tight I think he's about to break, he doesn't stop me.

I notice the way he fights it. On instinct, he tries to resist what's coming until finally, he lets out a guttural roar that the neighbors will definitely hear. I feel him release into the back of my throat, and I swallow. When I look up again, his eyes are wide and full of panic.

"Fuck," he stammers, tearing me away from the floor and onto his lap, where he kisses me so deeply I'm sure he's tasting himself. I keep my hands back while he rubs my body roughly from my ass to my shoulders. Then, I'm on my back, and he's tearing my pants off like a wild animal. When his mouth lands on my clit, I let out a strangled cry.

And just like I predicted, it doesn't take me long. I scream out his name as I wrap my legs around him, coursing through my climax and unable to breathe or move.

As we both come down from the high, panting and practically tingling over every inch of our bodies, he collapses on top of me. My hands stay above my head, but I want to wrap them around him so bad it hurts.

But I don't.

One step at a time.

Chapter Thirteen

RAFE

There's no rope on my door when I get off the elevator. Every day this week, I get off the elevator after work to a rope hanging on my door. It follows with dinner together and more boundaries being pushed in the bedroom. I feel myself falling without a parachute and the wind in my face is too fucking nice to worry about the landing. What will come of all of this, I don't know, but every night when I have her on my couch and in my arms, I can't find anything wrong with what we're doing.

I haven't completely let my guard down yet. Her

hands stay to herself, and my clothes stay on, but we're moving toward something that can't be undone. And I don't know if I should be feeling as good as I do about it.

I also haven't had much of a chance to ask about Ezra either. I assumed it would be easier to just lead into questions, but with the way things are going, it's like I'm putting the sex—or almost sex—at a higher priority than the questioning.

And that's how I know I'm really fucked.

Nothing—nothing—has ever come before my job. And now I'm letting Ezra slide because I'm too caught up almost nailing his sister. Sex is fucking evil.

For this reason only, I should be relieved that my doorknob remains empty when I get home, but it actually has me worried. My first assumption is that she is tired of my bullshit and tired of trying to help me with whatever it is I fucking need. But then I remember that I give that girl about five orgasms a day, so I can't imagine that's the problem.

When I knock on her door, it's only because I've learned from years on the force to go with my gut. Always. If something doesn't feel right, it's because there is something definitely not right.

Immediately, I hear her mumble, "Oh, fuck."

"Shelby?" I call, turning the door handle. It opens easily and I peek in. She's standing in the kitchen with her back to the door, and she turns herself away from me when I walk in.

"What's wrong?" My voice comes out in a heavy, demanding tone, and I don't mean it to. She sniffles, and I notice the half-empty bottle of wine on the counter next to her.

"I'm fine," she says, but I hear the difference in her voice.

"What happened?" Stepping in, I glance around the apartment, looking for whoever it is that has her crying in her house at night.

"No one is here, Rafe." When she turns toward me, I see the red spots across her nose and cheeks. Her eyes are wet and swollen. Quickly, I move toward her, eager to fix whatever is wrong with her. Did I do this?

"I'm fine, I promise," she cries.

"Then what is it?"

"I had a rough day at work, and I forgot to put the rope on the door. I'm sorry." She holds a tissue to her face and takes long breaths, but her lip still shakes. I don't say anything; what the hell would I say?

When she finally gets her tears under control enough to talk, she composes herself and looks at me. "I'm used to this job, I really am, but after so long, it just tends to become too much, you know? I'm strong, but I'm not made of ice, and you can only watch so many people die before you need to just have a good cry."

Jesus. What the fuck am I going to say to that?

"I can't imagine," I say.

"One of my favorites took a turn for the worse, and it never gets easier when the hope you want never comes. It just makes me so fucking mad, Rafe. Mad for them. Mad for their families. It's not fair." A sob slips through her lips as she cries into her wet tissue. Carefully, I reach my hands out to her arms, but she holds herself away from me. This is how accustomed she is to my needs. She won't lean in for a hug, even when she's the one who needs it.

Then, I get an idea. I can't give her the affection or support she wants, but I can offer her something that I think is even better.

"Put on some workout clothes and meet me downstairs," I say, pulling away and moving toward the door.

"What?" she asks, but I'm already out the door.

A few moments later she walks into my little makeshift gym in a pair of tight yoga pants and a sports bra that holds her breasts up, threatening to distract me from what I'm supposed to be focusing on.

"What are we doing?" she asks. She's not crying anymore, but her face is still swollen and tired looking.

"You have some stuff to work out." I pull her toward me and hold each of her hands in mine. Carefully, I slide on the glove, covering her knuckles and protecting her wrist. Her soft hands in mine make me want to kiss her. Instead, I tighten the velcro and put her hands out in front of her, guarding her face.

"Strike straight forward, and hit the bag here," I direct her, pointing to the worn out spots from my punches.

She doesn't hesitate before she lays three solid hits on the bag. The impact is strong, and I sense the frustration coming from her movement.

"Good girl." I step behind her, guiding her elbows in and her gloves back in front of her face. "Protect your face."

"But no one is hitting me."

"You need to keep your form anyway. Elbows in, fists up. Strike forward, and don't hyperextend your elbow." My fingers glide along the skin of her bare arms, and I feel the goosebumps erupting across her flesh. She glances back at me, and I refrain from kissing her.

"This is a lot of instructions for a stress reliever."

"Just punch the bag," I say. Then, laying a hand on her chest, I add, "Hit from here."

"You just want to touch my boobs," she replies with a straight face, and I can't hold back my smile. With a smack on her ass, I step back and let her punch all of the frustration from her day into that bag.

Watching her throw everything into this exercise, I try to take inventory of my feelings for her. Seeing her cry didn't make me happy. It awakened a sense of guilt. When did I stop hating her? Because now she makes me smile, and I find it hard to keep my hands to myself when I'm around her. And when I'm not around her, I'm miserable, watching the clock for when I can go home to the rope on my door.

She goes nuts on the punching bag for almost an hour. I'm sure her arms are scalding by the time she relaxes on the bench to grab a bottle of water. "Feel better?" I ask.

"Actually...yes." Her face is red, and sweat beads across her shoulders and back. I know how good it feels to throw punches and work up a sweat when life feels out of control. This is normally the place I come to when I need to work off the arousals and the inability to be vulnerable.

Right now, watching her body move in those tight workout clothes, it's doing the opposite. I keep thinking about what her lips felt like against my cock, and how freeing it was to watch her swallow it down, knowing that I shouldn't be ashamed of what I did. It made her happy, and after a few more nights of the same, she only wants it more.

I'm not a complete freak. And if I am, then she is too.

SHELBY

"Why do you do it?" he asks, handing me a towel and watching me rub the sweat off my back.

"Do what?"

"Your job. If it's so hard, then why do you do it?"

I have to take a moment to formulate a response. No one has ever asked me that before, but it's the question every hospice nurse prepares themself to answer. Why do we choose this life? To stand so near the veil between life and death.

Finally, I look up at him, easily lost in those dark eyes. "There's something so liberating about these patients. They're facing death, knowing they have only months, weeks, days left, and they're some of the most relaxed and happy people I've ever met." Sitting back against the wall a moment, I look at him, with his furrowed brow and angry stare. "Death isn't scary, and it's not the worst thing. Living an unhappy life... that's scary."

He seems to react to that, looking away like I've struck a nerve.

"I'm not unhappy, if that's what you're implying."

"I'm not implying anything."

"Then why are you looking at me like that?" he asks.

"Because I wish you'd talk to me. After everything, I just want to hear one thing, Rafe. Tell me one thing or just let me know that I've helped you."

"Is that what this is to you?" He stands up and approaches the large hanging punching bag. "You want to heal me?"

"I don't heal people. That's not my business, but if I can ease your pain, then yes, that's what this is."

"I'm not your fucking patient." I can feel him getting angry, and I don't want to upset him, so I put my hands up.

"I don't give my patients blow jobs," I say, and he laughs. What starts as a low chuckle builds into a heavy cackle, and I can't help but join in.

After a moment, the tension eases and I stand up, watching him while he throws punches at the bag. The rippled muscles in his back tense, and it becomes increasingly hard to not touch them. His skin is a shade or two darker than mine, a natural amber glow that shines under these lights and that thin sheen of sweat.

"Why did you say it like that?" he asks, grabbing the heavy bag and stopping its slow sway.

"Say what?"

"You just want to know that you've helped me," he says, and I can see a hint of shame in the way his eyes don't meet mine.

My shoulders soften as I step toward him, hugging the opposite side of the bag to be closer to him. "I didn't mean it like that, Rafe. But you won't even let me touch you, and I want to...so bad."

"There have to be plenty of other guys on Wicked who could give you what you want."

I know he doesn't mean that. I know he doesn't want to think about me with other guys, but he's being defensive, pushing his feelings aside so that I don't stomp on them.

"None of them would get me nearly as fired up as

you do," I say with a smile.

He smirks at me, and I almost remember a time—just a few weeks ago, that I wanted to punch him. And it's not gone, it's just changed. It brought us closer together, and now it's dangerously close to something else entirely.

"My birth parents were just really fucked up," he says before taking a couple quick punches. He doesn't punch with gloves like I do. His hands are loosely wound with gauze, but there is no wrist or hand support. I glance up at his face, backing away from the bag. What the hell do I say to that? I have no clue, so I let him have the space and silence he needs.

"They were a special brand of psychopath that thought that I...that we...were born so wicked that we needed to un-learn all of the deviant thoughts we were born with. They started with me."

He takes another quick six punch of the bag, blowing a deep breath out through his pursed lips.

"The abuse started when I was just eight. I remember the first time I had to kneel on thorns until I learned that touching myself was a sin. And I was never to let anyone else touch me either. No kissing. No hugging. Not ever."

His eyes meet mine, and I blink away the pooling tears. All I can think is that I first met him when he was seventeen. How had I not known then how recent this trauma was for him...and still is?

"I don't believe their bullshit, if that's what you're

worried about," he adds, avoiding my stare. "Even then, I knew they were deranged. But that shit stuck."

Quickly, he turns back to the bag. After a moment of watching him work, I step closer. I have myself convinced that if he'd just let me touch him, everything else would fall into place like dominoes. Then he could let himself be naked with me, then he could be inside of me. And then everything would be better.

I'm smarter than that. I know it's not that easy. I realize there is deep-seated trauma that will take him years if not his entire life to work out with a professional, but there's a nurturing part of me that is convinced if he just let me hold him, I could make his problems go away. We could work it out together.

"Rafe, I'm so sorry," I whisper, stepping closer. My eyes are on his chest, the dark tattoos scattered across his skin. "You let the tattoo artists touch you," I observe.

"He's my best friend. The kind that doesn't ask too many questions and always steps up when I need him to."

When the room grows silent, and he watches me bite my lip, I feel him step closer.

"Put out your hand," he commands, and like always, I listen. Holding my hand out, palm up, he takes it by the wrist. Flipping it over, he pulls me closer. With his eyes on my face, he gently lowers my hand to his chest.

My breath is caught in my throat. The skin under

my fingers is cool from the moisture and soft. Touching his body has me feeling even more connected to him, and as he watches my eyes while I press my hand more firmly against him, a hunger builds for more.

"It's not that I can't let people touch me," he says quietly. "I just don't like it."

My mouth has gone dry, so I wet my lips and nod. "I understand."

He motions for my other hand, and I give it to him. He places it against his chest as well, and then scoops his hands around my waist and pulls me closer until our bodies are flush. I'm lost in those dark eyes, so full of angst, but I'm starting to see so much more there. Rafe's walls are lowering for me, and I can spot the fear and vulnerability hidden behind them.

When his mouth touches mine, I melt into his arms.

Touching him hasn't been the domino effect that I hoped it would, but I'm starting to realize that it was never about the physical touch at all. He's letting me in because he trusts me, or he's starting to, and I feel like a monster because now that I know his secrets, I don't know if he should.

Chapter fourteen

RAFE

Her hand is draped across my arm when I wake up the next morning. That's not the weird thing. The weird thing is that it doesn't bother me. As my eyes open, I let my gaze focus on her fingers resting on my bicep. It seems so trivial, to allow her skin to touch mine, but I cut that part of me off so long ago.

I know I could have worked through the touching thing years ago, but it was always my self-sacrifice. My own special brand of torture.

It was all walls built up and armor suits from a young age. The shame they made me feel for shit I didn't even do yet...it was easier to push the world away than try to deal with that crap.

Now, she's in my bed, and her hand is on my body. And the shame hasn't brought me to my knees.

Maybe...just fucking maybe, I could do this.

She stirs, her eyes peeling open in the early morning light. Quickly, she pulls her hand away, like she did something wrong.

We didn't do anything after the gym last night. I invited her in so I could feed her something that wasn't wine, and while I was showering, she crawled into my bed. When I came out, she was snoring on my pillow.

I hate to admit how long I stood there and stared at her. She felt more comfortable in my bed than hers. She could have easily walked back to her own apartment.

"It's okay," I say, pulling her entire body against my bare chest. "I think I could get used to it." Her warm body against my skin is nice. She's in nothing but her sports bra and underwear, and I feel her smooth legs wrap around my body. A moment later, I feel her lips press against my chest, and goosebumps erupt everywhere.

"Is that okay?" she asks.

"You've had your lips on worse," I say, my voice low and gravelly from sleep.

She laughs against my chest, and a smile breaks out across my face.

"And I'd be all for that if I didn't have an appointment in an hour. I still have to shower."

"Yeah, I should get to work too." I haven't been paying enough attention to my job. Shelby's been a serious distraction, and it doesn't take long before I realize that her brother might be behind all of this, and everything between us could implode if it's on me to take him down—again.

It's that realization that prompts me to ask the question that's been waiting on my lips for days. As she crawls off the bed, I prop myself up on my elbow. "Hey, Shelby," I call.

She turns and smiles at me, finding my sudden formal greeting weird. "Yeah?"

"How's Ezra?"

She freezes. Her eyes dart around the room, not really focusing on anything as she picks up her pants and starts to pull them on.

"He's fine," she answers stiffly. "Why?"

There are so many more things I want to say. I should tell her that there has been some activity around his shop. But I can't bring myself to say anything other than, "Good."

She grabs her phone from the nightstand and stares down at me, still looking tense from my sudden awkward question. "Can we workout again tonight?" There's an eager look on her face, and it's a real fucking turn-on to see her working like she did last night.

"You're not sore?"

She flaps her arms slowly like a bird and lets out a

little wince. "A little, but I like it."

"You would," I say, smacking her ass.

Then I remember today is Thursday, and I promised Vic I'd fight tonight. "I can't. I have a fight."

What I expect is for her to look at me with some sort of disapproval. Instead, I look up to see an expression of excitement in her eyes. Her brows are raised, and she's biting back a smile.

The word no is already falling out of my mouth before she can even ask.

"Can I come?"

"Absolutely not," I say.

"Well, too bad you're not the boss of me. See you tonight," she calls before leaving my apartment. I'm on her before she can even reach the front door.

With my arms around her waist, I lift her off the ground, and her legs tuck in like a child as a squealing laughter escapes her lips.

"Why are you such a bad girl?" I growl, carrying her back to the bedroom.

She tries to fight, but it's a weak attempt. Still, she squeals with laughter as I drop her on the bed, her perfect round ass in the air.

"Don't make me get the rope," I bark, but even I hear the humor in my tone. She shrieks, but I notice the way she turns and glares back at me with her lip tight between her teeth as I rear my hand back and land a delicious smack right on her ass.

She lets out a cry, shoving her face into the bed.

"Are you going to listen to me?" I ask, pressing my weight on her to put my lips next to her ear.

"No," she whispers back. Then, she actually lifts her hips backward, inviting my palm as it lands another smack.

She groans again, almost sounding like she's getting off to the pain. Fuck, I better stop this little game now before we both end up late to work. Quickly, I lift her up and press my mouth to hers.

After pulling away, she almost looks drunk, with her red cheeks and ear-to-ear smile on her face. "Go to work, you little brat," I whisper, and she pouts.

"Fine."

Then I watch as she walks away, rubbing her ass and grinning like a fool.

SHELBY

When things get too good, I get worried. It's a natural reaction from having life never going my way growing up. When our dad left, when Ezra got arrested, when Mom remarried and moved on with her life...things just never ended up as well as we wanted.

So with as good as things are feeling with Rafe, I'm nervous. He's opening up, letting me in, and I feel like there is a momentum here that can't be stopped. In fact, I have a very good feeling that before long, he's going to let his guard down completely so that we can truly be together.

Physically and emotionally.

But underneath it all, I still have residual guilt over the way this all started. If I really wanted to break him now, like Ezra asked, I could.

I won't, but I could, and that's enough to keep my ear-to-ear grin laced with shame.

When I unlock my apartment door, still smiling from that sexy as hell spanking on Rafe's bed, and I find myself staring face-to-face with my brother, I'm not exactly surprised.

Having Ezra staring at me with a look of disappointment on his face is just the reminder I need that this is not a normal relationship with Rafe. We are not going to come out of this as a happy couple, walls torn down and together, riding off into eternal bliss. That is not in the cards for us. He's still the guy who turned my brother in and had him sent to jail for two years, and Ezra will never let me live with that if I choose Rafe.

"These walls are a little thin for an apartment I know you're paying a shitload for," he snaps at me.

"It's so we can hear the ocean waves," I answer without greeting him. "I have to get to work. I'm sorry I can't stick around and chat." As I move toward my bedroom, Ezra reaches out and takes my arm.

"What are you doing?" he snarls. "Tell me you're fucking him so you can break his heart into a million pieces, Shelby. Tell me this is your way of getting into his life so we can shatter him together. Just fucking tell me this is part of your plan of revenge and not you falling for him becasue what I heard through that wall was a hell of a lot of laughter, and you walked through that door with a smile on your face that said...I can't even say what it said."

Gritting my teeth, I pull my arm away. "I'm not the one who wants revenge, Ezra," I argue, even though I regret it immediately.

"Oh right," he says, and I can see him winding up. "Because you're not the one who went to jail."

"You went to jail for something you did, Ezra. You had plans to rob that jewelry store written all over papers in our fucking apartment. Don't forget that I almost went down with you!"

He looks like I slapped him, and I hate this. I hate fighting with him, letting out all of these things I've been holding in for years right now. I hate that I was high as a kite a moment ago, and now I feel lower than dog shit.

"I can't believe what I'm hearing," he says, flinching like it physically hurts to hear the truth. And I guess in a way it does.

"What he did was wrong, Ezra, but it was a long time ago. And we don't need revenge on him. What we need is to move on."

"I can see you've done that," he says, stomping toward the door.

"Ezra, stop!" I call after him. When he turns back toward me, I try to find the right words. Why am I defending Rafe? Why do I have these intense feelings for him when he did fuck us over so bad all of those years ago? How can I explain this to Ezra...that none of that matters to me anymore.

The only thing I won't say is that I'm sorry. I don't apologize for something I didn't do.

"I love you."

It's a stupid thing to say in the middle of a major fight, but Ezra is all I have. I don't talk to our mother much anymore, and things are still so new with Rafe. If I lose Ezra, I am alone. And that thought terrifies me.

I see the muscles in his jaw clench. He doesn't want to say it back, but he does anyway. "I love you too, Shel."

Then, he walks out my door, and I have to rush into my shower so that I'm not even more late than I already am.

Chapter fifteen

RAFE

If every time I was late to work, I was in this good of a mood, it wouldn't bother me in the least. In fact, I'd be late to work every day if it meant I could still taste Shelby on my lips when left every morning.

Fuck, this is getting too real. Too good. The shoe has to drop at some point, and I just keep waiting for it. I know I'm being an idiot. For all I know, she and Ezra have big plans for me that involve revenge and justice, and I'd probably deserve it, and at this point, I'll take it.

It's not like I ever wanted to do what I did. I didn't plan to turn in my best friend for a crime I was supposed to commit right along with him, but I just happened to get a call from Theo the night before we planned to raid the store, and he needed me. I had no choice but to come back to Wicked and abort the plan.

Ezra was pissed, and I could understand that, but Theo was my brother, in a sense. Enough that when he told me he was thinking about ending it all, I couldn't get in my car fast enough. Ezra wanted to go along with the job without me. There was no way the plan would have worked with one person. Without a lookout, he would have been killed. I knew that much.

When it was clear he wasn't going to abandon the raid, calling the cops was the only thing I could do to save his life. He wouldn't listen to me or Shelby, and I could be a stubborn asshole too.

I would regret that call for the next ten years, and not only because it ruined this new thing I had built with Shelby at the time, but because it let them down, and Ezra was just the kind of guy to hold a grudge. He'd never forgive me, and I had to live with that.

As I come out of my apartment, in less of a rush than I should have been in, I spot a familiar face about to climb into his car. Ezra looks up at me and scowls like I fucking stink or something.

He looks almost exactly the same. His blonde hair is still cut short, and his blue eyes have dark circles hanging below them, a sign that he doesn't sleep much and is probably under as much stress as he always was.

We stare each other down as I approach my bike. I hate the smug look on his face.

All I want to do is confront him about Mateo and what he has going on at the shop, but it's too soon for that. I can't raise any alarms, just yet, but it makes me sick to think that he's out and putting people in my town in trouble, and it's up to me to stop him.

Just when I think he's going to get in his car without incident, I hear him step closer. "Stay the fuck away from my sister."

Slowly I turn toward him. "Look, your sister is an adult. She can do what she wants."

"I'm serious, man." As he steps up, putting his finger in my face, I try to think of Shelby instead of clocking him right in that pretty face of his.

"You better get out of my face, Ezra."

"I've got my eye on you," he says, stepping back.

Now he's got me fired up, and all I'm thinking about is Shelby and Mateo and all of the other people he could hurt by being so reckless. "I don't know what you're up to, Ezra, but all of that shit from before is behind me now, and I don't want to deal with your shit around here."

Without another word, I climb on my bike and ride away.

SHELBY

"He's been talking more today," Mrs. Yan says as I take her husband's blood pressure. I can see the optimism in her expression, and it stings a bit, knowing I'm going to have to remind her that things are not going to get better. This is my least favorite part, and it happens almost every time.

"Darling, I would love a cup of coffee," Mr. Yan says to his wife. She looks at me with eyebrows raised, asking if that's okay.

The fun part of my job is that I generally get to say yes to almost any patient request because...why not? You want to go skydiving? Go for it. Want to have a full day sex marathon, do it! Want to finally try ecstasy? I'll load your IV for you.

Well, maybe that one is a little too illegal, but when Mrs. Yan asks if her dying husband is allowed to have coffee, I am reminded that people do not know how to do this. Sitting by the side of someone they love while they live their last days is not something they do very often, nor do they want to.

"Of course," I tell her with a smile.

Once she's in the kitchen, Mr. Yan touches my hand. "You look different."

I have to hide my blushing cheeks by turning toward my bag to put back my things. "How so?"

"I don't know. You seem happier. Brighter."

Turning back, I give him a warm smile. "Hm. It's

been a good week, I guess."

There's a knowing look in his eye, like he knows exactly what I'm talking about, but I can't tell my seventy-year-old patient that I'm in a good mood because I've been having orgasms for breakfast every day or that I was spanked this morning and it turned me on more than I expected it to, and I can't stop thinking about it.

"Oh I miss that look you have right there." Sitting back, he seems to retreat into his memory for a moment. I can't stop the laugh that bubbles up.

"How did you and Mrs. Yan meet?" I ask.

"We were high school sweethearts," he answers with a smile. "I didn't deserve her, but luckily for me, she put up with my cocky attitude, and once I realized that I would never get so lucky for as long as I lived, I asked her to marry me."

"That's so sweet."

Just as I turn away to finish packing up, he grabs my hand, and I almost panic, thinking he's in pain. When I look into his eyes, he's staring straight at me. "When you find someone who fits, go all in."

The look on his face is so serious that it almost chokes me up. Immediately, I think of Rafe, the easy comfort between us now. Waking up next to him and how easily he can put a smile on my face like this morning. It could be like this forever. I could go all in.

My appointment with Mr. Yan leaves me feeling in good spirits as I drive down the boardwalk toward my favorite coffee shop on the corner. I want to make things right with Ezra, and I'd like to do it in person. He usually works from home, but I figure I'll stop by the shop, hoping to catch him at work, but his car isn't parked near the orange brick shop called Wicked Goods. It will never get old how much everything around here is labeled Wicked, even though the town's real name is Wickett. It's like the locals have just accepted the nickname over the real one.

Then, I spot a familiar motorcycle parked out front.

Quickly, I pull into a free spot not far from the shop, something you can only find on a weekday in the fall. As I walk up to the shop, I stop when I see Rafe walking outside with a heavy box in his arms. A young boy follows behind him, and they both drop their boxes on the ground in front of an empty display stand.

When Rafe looks up, he catches me standing here with a quizzical look on my face. When I saw his bike I figured he might have stopped to pick something up. I didn't expect to find him working here with a teenage boy.

He smiles at me, a real-life smile, and I don't see a lot of those with Rafe so I drink it in like lemonade on a hot day. "Well, hello nurse," he croons, standing up and checking me out in my pink cherry blossom scrubs. "What are you doing here?"

"I was wondering the same thing about you," I answer, staring up at him, with the sun in my eyes.

"I was just helping my friend out. This is Mateo." He gestures to the boy who stands and holds his hand out to me. I bet the kid is only sixteen. With his dark hair and innocent looking eyes, I can imagine he is a lady killer for girls his age.

"Hi, Mateo," I answer, shaking his hand. "What are you guys doing?"

"We were just about to settle a debt," Rafe says as he pulls out his phone.

"He's trying to tell me that Mayweather was better than De la Hoya," Mateo adds in, shaking his head and looking at Rafe disapprovingly.

"It's adorable how clueless you are," Rafe fires back.

"Don't call me adorable!"

I can't help but laugh as they both start googling something on their phones. "The loser has to fill this display case by themselves," the boy says.

After a few moments, Rafe shouts, "See! Mayweather won in 2007. You don't remember that because you were still in diapers."

"One fight, old man! De la Hoya had a better record."

"How about this deal?" I say, interrupting their playful banter. "We all put this stuff on the display case together and I'll buy you both lunch at Gino's Pizza."

They easily agree but still throw sneers at each

other as we work.

Sitting across the table from Rafe and the teenage boy, I can't keep the smile off my face. I have no clue how these two know each other—boxing, maybe—but they seem to be close friends. Mateo is telling us about how he grew up in Juarez and what it was like moving here with his aunt and uncle. He seems like such a bright kid, and I can see the way his face lights up when I tell him I'm a nurse.

"What are you going to do after high school?" I ask, pushing the rest of my cheese slice aside.

His jaw clenches, and I notice the way he averts his eyes. "I have a scholarship to go to a university, but I have some stuff on my record now, and I might lose it."

Rafe leans forward, staring at the boy. "You didn't tell me that."

"Well, I didn't think you'd care," Mateo answers, still staring at his pizza.

I watch as Rafe's demeanor changes from angry to concerned. He doesn't say anything for a moment, but when the boy looks back up at him, I notice the subtle nod between him and Rafe. He's earning his trust, asking the kid to put faith in him, and I watch how easily the boy gives it to him.

Chapter Sixteen

RAFE

Since there's clearly no chance of me getting Shelby to stay home tonight, I walk into the gym with her on my arm. She's in black tonight, a pair of leggings so tight I can make out the cute dimples in her ass and a black shirt with a low-cut neckline that hangs between her tits making me want to reach out and run my fingers down between her clavicles.

"Do you ever get nervous?" she asks.

"Yeah, but that's kind of the point. You need the adrenaline rush. It keeps things from hurting too much."

We're watching a fight out back, and I keep Shelby

close to my side. It's not my place to tell her how to dress, but I know how my dick is reacting to her long body in all that tight black. I can only assume it's having the same effect on the other guys.

"What's the worst you've been hurt?"

"That night you found me," I answer, looking down at her with a wince.

"Why do you do it?" she asks. The crowd around the current fight boos when a limp body smacks against the ground.

"Hell if I know." The guys help the loser up, and I can see the dollar signs in Vic's eyes as he surveys the damage. When the unconscious guy comes to, there's pain on his face. That hurts like hell. "I guess I do it because as much as it hurts to lose, it feels fucking good as hell to win."

"Nolan!" a voice calls from behind me. When I turn, I spot Vic standing across the crowd, waving me over.

This time, I take Shelby's hand in mine as I wade through the crowd to where Vic sits on the raised patio, his table of bookies behind him, who I make it a point to not look directly at. I really couldn't care less about illegal gambling. I guess I probably should.

"Well, look who you brought again?" Vic's face lights up like a Christmas tree when his gaze falls on the woman on my arm. Vic is too fucking good-looking and charming for my comfort right now. He's the kind of guy who you never see with a woman, but you always see with a trail of them.

He's got a killer smile and a flirting skill that makes me want to punch the teeth right out of his face. He holds a hand out for Shelby and she takes it—with the opposite one holding mine, and he lifts it to his mouth to kiss it with a wink. I jerk her away with a scowl that makes him laugh.

"That's enough," I growl. Shelby looks up at me with a subtle smirk on her face, and I get the feeling she likes to see me acting jealous.

"She'll be safe with me while you're in the ring," Vic teases me. Fuck this guy.

"Looks like you're up," he laughs and points to the opponent waiting in the ring. I've fought this guy before, and I'm actually pleased to see him. He's not an easy win or an asking-for-a-beating opponent. He's a decent competitor. The only problem is…I don't hate the guy.

He's actually a fireman, and we work together a lot. He's the only hot-head who comes to these fights, and I know it's because he rides the straight and narrow otherwise. We all have our vices.

The problem with not hating him is that it makes it that much harder to win, and I have Shelby here to hopefully not watch someone beat the shit out of me.

I give her hand a squeeze and pull her aside so I can talk to her before leaving. Her eyes are nervous as she stares up at me. "Be careful," she mumbles.

I smile at her. "It's cute when you're worried about

me." At which she rolls her eyes.

"Stay up here by Vic, but don't let him get too close. Don't freak out if I get punched a couple times. I've done this a million times. I'm not going to get hurt like last time, but I want you to stay away from that crowd. They can get rowdy."

She steps up on her tip-toes and brushes my hair back. "It's cute when you're worried about me."

Then, I lean down and capture her mouth in a kiss. She clearly didn't expect it because she lets out a little yelp as my tongue invades her mouth. Melting in my arms, I hope she feels how fucking hot she makes me. And I really fucking hope Vic sees this kiss and keeps it in mind while she's up here with him.

As I pull away, she has an intoxicated look in her eyes. Then without a word, I walk straight for the ring. I don't need anyone seeing the hard on straining in my pants right now, but the tension sure as fuck is going to help when it comes time to win this match.

After wrapping my hands and bumping fists with my opponent, I keep Shelby in my peripheral vision as I go in for the first punch. It connects with his cheek just right, and he stumbles back.

He comes back with a smile on his face, and I manage to block and evade his next two swings. This fight is going to be tough, and I feel a moment of panic that it may end badly if this guy has been working out as much as it looks like he has been.

Just then, I hear a familiar voice yelling as I circle

the ring again. Keeping my eyes on the fireman, I listen to Shelby scream my name over the crowd.

She's cheering for me, and by the sound of her voice, she's really fucking into it.

SHELBY

I hate seeing him get hit, but I love watching him knock the other guy back. I thought I would hate this, but the way Rafe fights is sexy as hell. He doesn't just hit to beat the other guy, but you can see the turmoil he's fighting with every punch. It's not about winning for him. It's about beating up the demons inside as well.

When he spots me cheering for him, there's a new fire in his punches. He only takes one quick jab to the chin, but I notice how he dodges it enough that the guy's fist glides off his skin.

I bet it still hurt, and yet, it looks fun as well. Adrenaline rushing, pulse pounding, hitting someone as hard as you can and feeling the power in your punches. There's something about it that entices me, and I know how wrong that is. I'm supposed to help people, not want to beat them up.

Vic steps up beside me. "You know, we do have some lady fighters come out. Not often, but they do."

I shake my head at him. "This is definitely not for

me, Vic."

"You say that, but I see the way your eyes light up. This is what we were made to do, my darling. Fuck and fight."

I have to fight the blush in my cheeks. Vic is attractive, and if I wasn't already so overwhelmed with Rafe, I might have considered letting him make the moves on me, but since I enjoy turning him down so much, I glare at him.

"Well, one of those is already taken care of, thanks."

He grins at me, a knowing smile. "No, it's not. Not if the rumors about officer Nolan are true. Why do you think he loves to fight so much?"

When I glance back at the fight, I notice they're taking a break, getting water, and the other guy looks much worse off than Rafe. In fact, all I notice about Rafe is the moisture pooling on his brow. Otherwise, he looks pretty comfortable.

But Vic's words are sinking in. How does everyone know his secrets? It seems very unfair to me that everyone should feel the need to know what is so private to him. An overwhelming desire to defend him makes me turn toward Vic and say, "I assure you. The rumors are wrong."

Then I turn back toward the fight and just as they ring the bell, I scream for him again.

Only a few moments later, Rafe throws a hook that sends the other guy to the ground. When he doesn't get back up, the crowd erupts, and I can't help but yell along with them. Vic starts collecting his money, and I'm too distracted with rushing through the horde to get to Rafe.

He seems to meet me halfway, and before I know it, I'm in his arms and his lips are on mine again.

I don't even care that he's sweating or that I taste blood on his lip. When he pulls my body flush against his, I feel his heart beating in his chest, and it excites me.

He deepens the kiss, digging his fingers into my backside, and I'm not just hungry for Rafe anymore. I'm fucking starving.

When he pulls away, I whisper against his mouth. "Let's go home."

He doesn't answer, just turns on his heel and drags me back to his motorcycle.

Chapter Seventeen

RAFE

It's like falling down the side of a mountain, no brakes and nothing to stop us now.

I hope she doesn't mind if I take a shower when we get back because I feel disgusting, but as I climb on the bike and she wraps her arms around my waist, I realize she probably doesn't care. There was so much heat in that kiss, I know that the doors are wide open now and it's just up to us to walk through. And I'm ready.

Being with Shelby doesn't make me feel ashamed. It doesn't make me want to punch a hole through the wall—not anymore. When I'm with her, I'm not alone.

She's riding every wave of pleasure with me, and it's like the only two people who exist are her and me.

As we pull up to the apartment, she barely lets go of me. She takes my hand as we walk inside. She presses herself against me, kissing me as we ride up to the fourth floor. And I kiss her back, shoving her against the wall, barely even flinching as her hands touch my chest.

"I need a shower," I groan as we stumble into my apartment, our lips still locked. She starts tearing off my jacket.

"No, you don't," she mumbles against my lips.

Hoisting her up by her ass, I shove her body against the closed door, grinding myself against her. There's no stopping us. I feel it coming.

But what if I panic? What if I get this far and when the time comes, some buried trauma comes back and makes me freak the fuck out. What if the damage is so bad that I don't have any control over my reaction to this. I can't fucking hurt her, and I just need a minute to think.

"Really, I need a shower," I complain, kissing her neck.

"I could come with you," she gasps.

"Just give me ten minutes, okay?" I ask, setting her down and kissing her forehead. She finally agrees and lets me walk away. "Get yourself a drink and don't go anywhere."

When I get to the bathroom, I stop in front of

the mirror and stare at the reflection there. For one, I look like shit. Broken lip, sweat mixed with dirt on my forehead, bags under my eyes, and a layer of anxiety hidden beneath it all. Is this what Shelby sees when she looks at me? Is this the person she wants in her bed?

Pushing the thought away, I climb into the shower and turn the heat up as high as it will go. The scalding water against my back brings back memories that, instead of pushing away, I let them rise up. For a brief moment, I stare at the memory of my parents shoving me into that nearly boiling water to cleanse me of my wicked desires. For what? Because I touched myself, because I woke up with morning wood like every other guy my age? They infused me with a shame before I was old enough to know anything else.

And here I am, ready to let myself get close to someone who I actually trust, and it's time to face that memory and tell it to fuck off.

Taking a long breath, I brace myself. This terrifies me, but it's never not going to terrify me, so I have to accept the fact that at least I'm facing it with someone good.

As I step out of the shower, I wrap a towel around my waist and step into the bedroom. She's standing against the window, looking out at the water. Tucking my towel around me so it doesn't fall, I step up behind her, hoping we can recover the passion from earlier and I didn't kill the mood by needing a few minutes to think.

Pulling her hair back, I trail kisses across her shoulders and down her back. Letting out a long moan, she leans back into my arms. "We can take it slow," she whispers.

After peeling her shirt from her body, my lips find the grooves of her spine, kissing each vertebrae. "I've taken it slow my entire life. I'm fucking tired of slow. Right now, I want to devour you. I want to strip away your clothes, and I want to make you scream my name while I fuck you."

She gasps, arching her back, pressing her ass into my cock.

Getting on my knees, I turn her body. My tongue trails a soft line just above the hem of her pants. Then, I carefully pull them down, taking a long look at the black lacy panties in front of me. I press my face against the black fabric, and she lets out another moan that feels like a shockwave to my painful erection.

"Don't tease me, Rafe," she cries, digging her fingers into my hair.

"What do you want me to do?" I whisper against her sex.

She bites her lip, hesitating, and I know she's not used to dirty talk, but I meant what I said. I want everything. All the filthy thoughts in her head belong to me.

"Say it, Shelby. Tell me what you want." My thumb

draws circles around her clit, and I watch the goose-bumps erupt along her legs and belly.

"Fuck me, Rafe," she cries, and when I look up at her, her pupils are dilated and so full of desire, it makes a smile stretch across my face.

Standing up, the towel still fastened in place, I pick her up and carry her to the bed. Her legs are wrapped around me as I drop her weight on the mattress, leaning down to kiss her. I love how she tastes, and I nearly get lost in the way she pulls my bottom lip between her teeth.

While I'm up there, I manage to unclasp her bra and pull it away. As I move my mouth toward her perky, pink nipples, she grabs my face. "Now, Rafe. No foreplay. Fuck me, now."

My cock jolts again. My heart races in my chest. Leaning back, I pull her panties down her legs, and watch as she squirms, needy and ready on the bed. She looks so fucking beautiful in this moment it hurts, and there's an ache in my chest when I think about what this all means. She knows how heavy this moment is for me. The vulnerability she's showing doesn't go unnoticed.

I must hesitate for a moment too long because she sits up and touches my cheek. "Do it for me, Rafe. I need it," she moans, pulling my chest forward and placing a kiss on my heart.

This is how she changes everything for me. She knows I can't stop myself if I'm just doing it to please her.

Her fingers pull at the towel around my waist, dropping it to the floor, and she keeps her eyes on my face as I reach for the condoms in the side table drawer. In a rush, I rip one open and roll it on.

"Lie down," I command and she listens. As my fingers run along the slick arousal pooling near her entrance, she squirms again. She wants me. She needs me.

Lifting her legs under my arms, I position myself, and her eyes meet mine. Just as her lips part, I shove myself in, sliding as far in as I can go.

My mind goes blank. There are no thoughts, just the tight, warm sensation of being a part of her. I become an extension of Shelby, and the pleasure is almost too intense.

Her head falls back as she groans. "Yes, Rafe."

Hearing my name on her lips makes my hips jolt forward, and my body moves on its own. There are no painful memories, no traumatic stress—just the feel of her body swallowing me whole, and it's fucking heavenly.

She squirms, urging me to rear back and slam into her again. She writhes, gripping the sheets in her fists as I do it again and again.

When I pick up the momentum, her breathing gets shallow, and I focus solely on the pleasure it brings her. Making her come is my only goal.

It's just when I feel her body tense, her legs

clamped around my waist and her breathing stopped completely, that I lose control. My orgasm won't stop. And I don't know the moment when I collapse on top of her, but when I finally open my eyes, she's holding me against her chest, stroking my back.

My heart is knocking against my chest, and I swear I see stars floating around my vision. Turning to look at her face, I notice the moisture in her eyes.

There are a lot of fucking crazy thoughts coursing through my mind at the moment, and I know I could just blame it on the post-sex hormones or some shit because I'm feeling a lot of very intense things about Shelby, and by the way she's looking at me, she feels them too.

SHELBY

I've never climaxed so hard during sex in my life. Scratch that...I've never come at all during sex. But Rafe unravels me. He tears apart everything I thought was real and reconstructs it in a new light. I don't recognize anything when I'm with him, and it's the only explanation as to why I haven't felt happier.

This sex wasn't about first times or losing virginity or anything like that. Rafe is way too hard to see through that lens. This was about destroying demons and doing it together. It was about facing fears and sending a big old fuck you to the people who hurt him. The ones who do not control him anymore. And that is so much more powerful than any first time melodrama.

For a long beautiful moment, he's staring at me, and I feel so connected to him. It's scary how intense it is, and my heart tries to warn me, but I can't help it. He consumes me. My whole life lately has been nothing but Rafe, and it's all I want.

But then he stands up and walks to the bathroom without another word, and worry creeps in. I don't want him beating himself up in there, letting those demons win. So I stand up, letting the blood drain back to my legs which are still tingling from that explosive orgasm.

I give the door a simple knock. "Tell me you're good."

"I'm good," he answers in his deep gravelly voice.

Not knowing what to do, I turn back to his bed and decide to crawl in. I don't want to leave him, and he hasn't minded me sleeping over before. I also decide to stay naked, hoping that once won't be enough for him. I could do that all night. Not to mention, trying out all the positions to see his reaction sounds like so much fun at the moment.

I hope I'm sore when I go to work tomorrow.

When he finally comes out of the bathroom, he stops at the end of the bed and stares at me like there's something he wants to say. For a moment, I have this irrational fear that he's about to dump me and send me home. His first time and he's already jumping into the hit it and quit it mentality. Seems a bit extreme right out the gate.

"What's wrong?" I ask.

"I don't want to talk about it."

He's hardened since before, a natural reaction for Rafe as I've come to know, but I can't say I blame him. He's probably working through a lot of emotions and feeling super vulnerable about it. Normal people would struggle with opening up about that, so it's no surprise that Rafe sure as hell won't.

"Good, because the last thing I want to do is talk," I reply, opening the sheets next to me so he gets the hint. Judging by the still rock hard erection jutting straight out, he's ready for round two.

He hesitates for a moment, but before I can start to get anxious about it, he walks over and climbs in. I still try not to reach for him unless I know he's okay with it. He's loosened up about the touching rule, but I know it hasn't completely gone away.

So I wait for him to reach for me, which he does. Hooking a hand around my waist, he pulls me toward him, positioning me under his body. Gently, he nudges me knees open and rests between my legs. Then, he leans down hovering his face inches above mine and staring into my eyes for a second before kissing me.

When I feel the head of his erection against my clit, warmth courses through my body. It's amazing how ready I am just after doing it once, but with him, I want to go crazy. I want all of the things I didn't know I wanted. Tie me up, talk dirty to me, make it rough and make it sensual. It doesn't translate to anything other than two people who trust each other, which considering how all of this started, is a very stupid thing to do.

When he reaches for the side table drawer again, I grab his arm. "Feel me without it," I blurt out. This is next level trust here, and I can see the same thought in his eyes as he stares at me.

"I'm clean, and I'm on the pill."

"Are you sure?" he breathes, and he asks it in a way that tells me he's really praying I'm sure. When I nod, he leans back in to kiss me again.

With our lips still tangled, he presses himself inside me again. The way his body melts into mine and the husky groan that comes out of him tells me that he enjoys it much more without the rubber, and I have to bite back the smile on my face. I want him to feel everything, and I want him to enjoy it. Free of shame or pain and not beating himself up or trying to run.

Suddenly, I find myself wanting to give him everything I have, including my heart.

Chapter Eighteen

RAFE

"Keep your elbows in," I tell her again before she punches the pads I'm holding again. Shelby is a natural, but I'm not surprised. Boxing isn't about strength or skill. It's about fire, and you can't practice that. She has it naturally. I saw it then, and I see it now.

Maybe it's from years of feeling neglected by her mother or the struggle of being a nurse that can never truly heal her patients, but Shelby punches with more than muscle.

Plus the sight of her in her sports bra, glistening with sweat, with her biceps and traps flexing with every swing...it's sexy as fuck, and it's exactly what I'll be thinking of when I take her upstairs. I planned to workout too, but fuck that now.

Absolutely nothing changed after we fucked yesterday. I'm not looking at sex like it's something transformative, and I love Shelby's acceptance that I don't want to talk about it. Although I see her holding back. She wants me to talk about it, and before we even did it, she tried suggesting that I talk to someone professionally. I already told her that doing that would put shit on my record that I wasn't comfortable with. It was bad enough my parents screwed me up so bad I didn't let anyone touch me until a month ago. I wasn't going to let them ruin my career and chain me to a desk for the rest of my service too.

"What would you think of me fighting at the gym?" she asks.

I can't hide my reaction as my face contorts into a scowl. "What are you talking about?"

She smiles. "I think Vic was suggesting it last night. He said he has girls fight sometimes."

"No," I answer, sending her a harsh glare.

She holds up her gloves in confusion. "So, I get to watch you get beat up, but I can't do it? That's not fair. Also, I'm sorry if I sounded like I was asking permission."

What is this girl doing to me? That smart mouth of hers is going to get her in trouble. "Watch that mouth," I mutter, and I notice the devious look in her eye before she takes another swing, this time a bit harder than before. After a moment of silence, I ask, "Do you want to?"

She takes a second to think about it before nodding her head. "I think I do."

For a moment I let myself consider it. There aren't a lot of girls fighting, especially in the lot fights, and Maggie is the only one in her weight class, but Maggie fights with something stronger than fire. She fights dirty, and she doesn't give a fuck. The thought turns my stomach, picturing Shelby up there, taking hit after hit, and I clench my jaw just thinking about it.

"The answer is still no," I say before tossing the pads on the bench and picking up my gloves to start taking swings of my own. She's got me worked up now.

"Again, I'm not asking permission."

I start throwing swings at the bag. One, two, three, four.

"Are you ignoring me now?" Her chest is still heaving from the exertion, but she's not stepping back.

"No," I answer. One, two, three, four.

"This is how you solve all your problems? Don't face them, just punch something?" I knew she'd eventually start pushing me to open up. It's not enough that we have a good time together and the sex is good, but she's trying to fix me, and it's getting a little more intense every day.

"I'm not solving my problems," I argue. "I'm ignoring them."

"Oh, even better," she quips before turning away,

and something about her sarcastic remark makes me snap. Tearing off my gloves, I catch her around the waist, putting my mouth by her ear.

"What did I tell you about that smart mouth of yours?" I whisper.

There's a subtle smile curling up her lips. "What are you going to do about it?" she teases me.

"Put your hands on the wall," I command, and she bites her lip. "Spread your legs."

She does as I say, and I glance up. The wall is one long mirror so that when I stare up at the reflection, I see her—hands against it, ass held up in front of me, lust in her eyes. Then I see myself, standing behind her, and I know the dirty thoughts racing through my mind.

I want to spank her ass so hard it leaves a handprint, even through her clothes. I want to tear off her pants and fuck her hard, so hard she screams. I want to dominate her and let her feel how much she belongs to me.

The painful erection in my pants wants it too. What the fuck is wrong with me?

This is wrong. So wrong. These thoughts in my head...it's like I want to hurt her.

"Rafe," she murmurs, sending her hips back so she grinds her ass against my groin. I grip her hips hard to stop her movement. "Look at me," she whispers, and my eyes cast down from my own reflection to hers.

"What are you thinking?" she asks.

I almost don't answer her, but the words slip out anyway. "I'm thinking about what I want to do to you."

Her lips part, and I see the lust in her eyes again. "Tell me."

I don't move. I can't tell her these things. It would scare her away, which is exactly why I should. She should be afraid of me, and I should make her leave, but I can't bear the thought of being without her again. Being alone with these fucking thoughts.

"Better yet," she whispers. "Show me." She straightens up, takes her hands away from the wall and peels down her yoga pants, revealing her bare ass before bending back over and putting her hands back where they were.

She's tempting me. I remember the warnings. There would be women who would tempt me, and I had to be strong enough to resist. I had to know the shame of wanting to give in to temptation, and then I had to walk away.

My jaw clenches as my hands slide along the length of her ass. I don't know what makes me do it, maybe my desire to give in to temptation, maybe the need to teach her a lesson or maybe both, but I draw my hand back and land a harsh smack against the flesh of her backside. She yelps, and it both turns me on and revulses me at the same time.

"Do it again," she moans, pressing her hips back. So I do, this time on the opposite cheek. She seems to cry out in both pain and pleasure and it sends a tick down my spine.

My hand rubs the spot that is now turning red, and she senses me hesitate when I'm sure she's ready for me to make my next move, but I'm frozen. Yesterday, my mind was so clear, but now it feels like a hundred voices all vying for my attention—for control, and I don't know which one to listen to.

"Whatever you're feeling," she says, drawing my eyes to her again. "I want you to take it out on me."

I swallow. Why is she doing this to me? Why does she want me to hurt her?

She's tempting me, that's why. She's trying to turn me into the twisted fuck I've been fighting against for years. And she has no idea what she's releasing.

Grabbing her hips, I slam my body against hers, grinding my erection along the crevice of backside. She moans, writhing from the friction through my shorts.

With a quick flick of the waistband, my cock bounds free, and I don't hesitate before burying myself deep into Shelby's warm folds. She lets out a shocked moan. A shiver ripples up her spine as I freeze. I let her body adjust to the size for a moment, but I'm not trying to be gentle. She wanted me to be rough, so when her hooded gaze falls on mine in the reflection, I start to move again, this time picking up speed and slamming so deep, I know she feels every inch.

Her cries can probably be heard on the top floor.

It doesn't take me long before I'm unloading inside her, feeling her pussy clench around me just be-fore her knees start to weaken beneath her. Quickly, I scoop her up in one arm and hold her against my body, still buried deep inside.

For a short moment, I feel good. The residual ec-stasy has me in its grips until it doesn't and then I start to feel bad. Very fucking bad.

"Why are you doing this to me?" I mutter, find-ing her eyes again in the mirror. There's a moment of surprise in her eyes.

"Doing what?" she answers.

I don't reply. Instead, I let her go and pull out, feel-ing the cold lonely air on my dick, which is not deflat-ing fast enough. She pulls up her pants, and I see the confusion on her face. Last night, we ended sex with cuddling and pleasantries. And I don't know what's gotten into my head tonight, but what we just did has me feeling less like a man and more like an animal.

She reaches for me, and I flinch, turning to pick up our stuff, ready to be in the shower and far away from the new awkwardness in the room.

"Talk to me," she says, reaching for my face, and on reflex, I grab her wrist, squeezing it in my hands so hard she flinches. Immediately I let go.

I'm not this guy. I don't hurt people, not people who don't want to be hurt.

"One minute you want me to fuck you senseles and the next you want to talk?"

"You're deflecting, Rafe."

"Don't talk me like I'm a fucking patient."

"I'm not," she argues. "I'm talking to you like someone who cares about you."

"If you cared about me, then why do you do that? Why do you push me? Why can't you just listen to me?"

"Is this about me fighting? Because I'm not being obedient enough for you?"

"It's about you tempting me," I blurt out, and it was the wrong thing to say. I know that, but it's the thought at the forefront of my mind, and no matter who put the thought there, it was the first thing to fall out of my mouth when I opened it.

She looks offended, and I don't blame her. Resting back on her heels, I watch her purse her lips and glare at me, unafraid and angry.

"I shouldn't make excuses for you, but I know you didn't mean that."

My shoulders slump, and I let out a painfully long sigh. "Fuck," I groan as I drop onto the bench, lowering my head into my hands.

She sits next to me. "Maybe we're going too fast," she breathes, and for the first time ever, I want her to touch me. Just put a hand on my back or something, but I don't deserve it. I don't deserve to feel comfort.

But she doesn't because she's afraid of me.

I don't speak for a long time and she leans in, holding herself just inches away. "Whatever is going on in your head," she whispers. "It's not going to go away.

You didn't do anything wrong," she says, reaching for my shoulder. I don't react when her fingers touch my skin. In fact, I lean into the contact.

"The shit in my head is dark, Shelby."

"They're making you think that, Rafe."

She's being too good, too kind. If she knew the truth...

I turn my head toward her and look her in the eye, hoping she catches the severity of my words. "I wanted to hurt you."

There's a flinch in her expression, and I know it scares her to hear me say that.

"I liked being rough with you...maybe so rough it didn't feel good to you."

Shame pools in my gut as I voice these dark things, knowing that I have just ruined every good thing we started. Then, she shocks the shit out of me by scooting closer instead of moving away. Her hand on my shoulder moves to my cheeks as she pulls my face toward hers.

"Don't you try to be the nice guy now, Rafe Nolan. I'm the one who knocked on your door looking for a hate-fuck. I'm the one who tied a rope on your door. You think you're the only one with dark desires? A girl doesn't mouth off on purpose just to get spanked if she doesn't want it rough. So stop beating yourself up. If you're fucked up, then so am I."

She presses her lips softly against mine, and I feel something shatter in my chest. It's like she's crawling inside of me and warming up all of the frozen shards of what used to be my heart.

"I'm never going to be normal, Shelby. I'm never going to bounce back from what they did, and every time we fuck, I'll feel this way."

"It doesn't have to be that way," she whispers. "You can heal, Rafe. Maybe you'll never be 100% but who is?"

Pulling away, I already feel disappointment that I can't give her what she wants. "I already told you I can't talk to a shrink. It will ruin my career."

"But it's ruining your life," she answers, pulling me back to her.

She has a point, but she just doesn't understand how impossible this is for me. After a tense moment, she seems to relax. "Can you start with me?"

"No," I answer. If I tell you all the dark shit in my head, then you'll know, and it's not really stuff I want you to know."

"I understand," she replies, and I wonder if she's thinking the same thing. "What about the guys at the shop? Your friends?"

I almost argue back that they have lives of their own now. Murph is about to start a family, and Logan has his own mental shit to deal with, but I don't want to bog her down with excuses and arguments. So, I nod and promise her that I will try.

After we pack up the gym, I glance at the mirror again, and I feel a bolt of regret that I couldn't just enjoy what turned out to be a pretty fucking hot round against the mirror. Maybe that's the motivation I need. If I can get shit right in my head, I'll be able to do all of the things that make her look at me like she did when I had her bent over like that.

As we take the elevator up together, her still holding my hand, the gnawing feeling comes on when we both have to face whether we will go into our apartmnts alone or together. We're always at my apartment, and as fucked up as tonight was, I don't want to let her go yet. So as we approach the two doors, I put a hand out.

"Give me your keys."

She glances up at me with confusion on her face, but she still does what I tell her, a hint of mischief in her eye. Taking the keys, I unlock her door, and pull her in for a kiss, holding her body against mine as we walk in.

"I want you to ride me in your bed tonight," I mumble against her lips.

But then I register the presence of someone else in room and throw Shelby behind me as I turn to find Ezra standing in the living room looking fucking livid as hell.

SHELBY

"Ezra—" I jolt. Quickly, I step toward my brother, but he isn't looking at me. There's a scowl on his face and he's laser-focused on the man behind me.

"You," he growls. I've never seen Ezra look so angry.

"Ezra, calm down," I say, stepping closer. He can't be that mad that I'm with Rafe. He knew I was spending time with him. He shouldn't be so surprised.

"Calm down?!" he shrieks at me. "He's doing it all over again, Shelby. He's doing what he did ten years ago just to torment me! Or to get me out of the way so he can have you all to himself."

"What are you talking about?" I ask.

Rafe is standing quietly behind me, but by his posture, I can tell he's just as confused as me but as angry as my brother.

"He wants me to go back to prison, but this time he has to frame me for it!"

"You're not making any sense," I reply.

"They served a warrant at the shop today," he snaps. "They ransacked my entire inventory, scared the shit out of my employees, and you know what they found?"

I glance back at Rafe who suddenly wears a blank expression. He knew about this warrant. It's written all over his face.

Ezra pauses a moment staring at Rafe too, still seething with anger, his jaw clenched. "Nothing. They found nothing!"

"How is this my fault?" Rafe barks as he steps forward, chest puffed up. Quickly, I get between them and try to calm them down before they start fighting.

"Tell me you didn't request that warrant." Ezra stands his ground, his fists clenched at his sides.

"I'm a cop. It's my job," Rafe snaps back.

"You're a shitty fucking cop!"

"Enough!" I shout between them. Before long our neighbors will be knocking on the doors or calling the police.

Ezra seems to relax a little and paces the room, but I'm still desperate to separate them before something tragic happens. Just when I think he's about to calm down, he steps back toward Rafe. "You and I have business to settle. And I think it's time we settle it your way. Friday night at Vic's."

"No!" I shout, but he doesn't listen.

Instead, he continues. "If you win, I won't get in your way. If I win, you never see Shelby again."

"Ezra!" I scream, and I can't believe what I hear next.

"Fine," Rafe barks, and I spin on my heels to look at him, shock written all over my face. He did not just agree to fight for me. He wouldn't do that. Fight my own brother.

Nevermind the fact that Rafe is a shoe-in to win this fight and could probably seriously hurt Ezra, who is a big guy but has no fighting training except for maybe what he learned in prison, which can't be much.

As Rafe's eyes meet mine, he doesn't apologize. His stare is hard, like the man I reunited with a month ago, not the man who bared his soul to me today and last night.

A burning anger courses through me as I walk

toward the door, opening it and staring at the two of them. "Both of you. Out!"

Neither one of them puts up a fight, and I can't look them in the eye as they pass through. If these two idiots want to beat each other up for me, fine. They can do it. But I made absolutely no part of that bargain, and I won't promise to be around when it's over.

Chapter Nineteen

RAFE

On Friday, I stop by the shop to check on Mateo before heading to the gym. He and his aunt seem a little shaken up by the raid, but they seem fine now. It does little to settle the guilt in my chest. I've been neglecting work lately, and to be honest, I forgot I put in the paperwork for that warrant. I gave the chief hell the next day for sending someone else to serve a warrant I requested, but he was quick to point out that I've been less than focused lately.

So it's a good thing this shit ends tonight.

I'm going to knock Ezra down a peg, and then Shelby, and I can move on without the drama. She hasn't spoken to me since the fight, but I know she'll come around. I'd rather ask for forgiveness than permission at this point.

As I make my way through the crowd, I spot her first. She's looking pissed, standing next to Ezra who looks ready to rage. I'm headed straight for them to call this whole thing off when Vic snaps me up by the arm.

"I have a very bad feeling about tonight," he says without any other greeting. "And I trust my gut, Rafe. When I have a bad feeling it's because something bad is about to happen." Although I know very confidently that Vic doesn't do drugs, he's showing the paranoia of an addict.

"It's fine. This is about to be an easy win. I won't hurt him too bad."

"Then why is everyone betting against you?" His words stop me dead in my tracks.

"What are you talking about?"

"Everyone's talking about this guy. I mean, look at this crowd," he says with panic in his eyes. And that's when I notice that the gathering is about three times as strong as it normally is. What the hell is going on?

Turning my back on Rafe, I stalk through the crowd toward Ezra who is looking a little too smug for my taste.

Stepping up to his face, I don't hesitate. "What the fuck is going on?"

He smiles. "You're not nervous, are you?"

"Who are all these people?"

"Oh you didn't think you were the only one training,

did you?" That's when the wheels start turning. These people aren't like Vic's crowd. They're younger, rowdier, and a new buzz on energy runs through the crowd.

"What are you talking about?" Shelby chimes in. The way she's clutching her fingers in front of her tells me that she's as clueless as I am.

"I wanted to surprise you. I've been fighting every week over at Chief's. I just wanted to make sure I'd be a fair opponent for Rafe."

"What?" she shrieks.

The blood starts to boil under my skin. Chief's is another gym closer to Newport. They've been shut down more than once because, unlike Vic's, the crime doesn't stop at illegal betting. I personally answered a call there a few years back, and I remember the bad feeling I got from the place. If Ezra learned to fight there, he did not learn to fight clean.

"We're not doing this," I say before Ezra can say another word.

He lets out a raucous laugh. "Oh no, you don't. We made a deal, Nolan."

"I don't care. I'm not going to fight you, Ezra." Watching Shelby's face for any sign that she's relieved, she hardly reacts.

"No, this is bullshit. I've been looking forward to kicking your ass for years. Ten years to be exact." Ezra steps past Shelby to puff up his chest toward me.

"Is that what you want, Ezra? You want to hit me? So you've been spending your time at the seediest place in town, so you can rub elbows with the criminals and learn to fight dirty?"

"I want to do more than hit you," he snaps back.

"Because I saved your ass from getting killed that night. I knew how these things went down, Ezra, and I tried to talk you out of it. I begged you to wait for me, but you wouldn't, and you left me no fucking choice," I argue back, feeling myself getting hot with anger.

"You're so full of excuses, Rafe. Nothing is ever your fault."

"I'm not fighting with you like this, not in front of Shelby," I answer, but he doesn't slow down.

Just then, Vic appears at my shoulder. "I've got you on in fifteen."

I can't look at Shelby, but I feel her eyes on me. We may have been happy just a few days ago, but all of that feels fucked now. Still, I want to wrap my hands around her waist and pull her close. I want her to kiss me the way she did last time she watched me fight.

"I won't watch this," she mutters as she walks away.

"Stop," I command, but for once, she doesn't listen. Ezra doesn't move to follow his sister, so I do. She's heading quickly toward the parking lot, and I grab her arm before she can cross the street. "What do you want me to do?"

"Where do I start?" she says without looking at me.

"What's that supposed to mean?"

Spinning on her heels, she faces me. "It means you want to fight your way out of everything, Rafe. Why can't you just talk to him? Ezra is mad, yes, but he's also impulsive and reactionary. We know this. But you...you won't talk to him, you won't talk to me. For ten years you let us hate you when you could have just explained why you did what you did. You could have apologized! Shown up for his hearings. You could have been there for me so I wasn't so alone. And now...you want me to trust you, but I don't even know you, Rafe. I don't know you and somehow..."

"Somehow what?" I breathe, waiting desperately for her next words, knowing what it is she's on the verge of saying but not quite sure how I feel about it.

"No. I'm done being the one who talks." With that, she turns on her heels and walks away. I should follow her, leave all of this behind and take her home to say all the things I need to say, but I don't. Why? Because this is my default. This is what I know how to do. I walk away.

And for the first time ever, I feel like shit about it.

When I get back to the fight, Ezra is waiting. He's bouncing on the balls of his feet. I decide at that moment as I peel my shirt off that I will let him hit me. At least once, I'll let him have a good swing at my face, and judging by the evidence that he's been working out, it's going to hurt like hell. I don't throw fights, and I hate those who do, but this isn't throwing it. It's just a good hit that I know he wants and I deserve.

So after we go through the usual spiel with the off-duty ref, I don't dodge, and Ezra swings, making painful contact with my chin. It hurts more than usual, probably from the lack of adrenaline. My heart just isn't into the fight tonight. If I fight better hating someone, it makes sense why this fight isn't doing it for me. I don't hate Ezra. Even if he is impulsive and wild. He may not be my friend anymore, but I still can't hate him.

For the next ninety seconds, I dodge and block every swing and I pull my punches, only making contact twice.

"I see what you're doing," he groans when they ring the first bell. "It's pathetic."

I don't reply. I'm still thinking about Shelby and how stupid all of this is. I should be at home with her. I have two more rounds of this to get through and then I'll be fast on her heels, waiting outside her door. I'll sleep there if I have to.

"You think she gives a shit about you?" Ezra calls over to me with a sneer.

I don't answer because those words do feel like a punch as it is. Yes, I did think she gave a shit about me. But I brush him off. He's just trying to get me worked up.

"She's just fucking you to get close to you, so we can find the thing you love and take it from you. To fuck you over the way you fucked us over."

When my eyes find him, something he said strikes a nerve. He didn't tell me anything I didn't already know. Of course Shelby was using me to get what she wanted. In the beginning, so was I.

But he said, "find something you love and take it from you."

Clenching my jaw, I stare at him. A second later, the bell rings and we move toward each other. Neither of us swing as we circle the center of the ring.

"I think I know exactly what you love," he laughs. He's taunting me, and I just have to ignore him.

I take a swing, but he dodges it and comes up with an uppercut to my side that knocks the wind out of me. The crowd reacts, and I move away to get my head right before he can swing again. He can't throw a strong left. I've caught onto that much, but his words are still swirling around in my head, and I can't make a plan.

"I didn't need to take that from you, did I? I knew you'd lose her all by yourself." He sneers, and I go in for another hit to the face. This time, I make contact with his cheek, but he swings back at me, and suddenly, we're wrestling.

I hear yelling before he shoves me away and swings again, smacking me so hard against the side of my head, I crumble to my knees.

"Rafe!" she screams just before pure chaos breaks out. Quickly, I get back up even though I don't hear the ref counting. There are red and blue lights reflecting off the cement.

"Ezra, stop!" she screams again, and I look up for her. Why did she come back? I didn't want her to see this. Jumping to my feet, I try to find her, but everyone is scattering around.

My vision blurs, and I turn just in time to see Ezra's angry eyes as his fist comes down on my face.

Then, everything goes black.

SHELBY

I saw the patrol cars before I pulled off the street. In a panic, I turned around and rushed back to the lot just in time to see them flash their lights and the crowd scatter.

By the time I get to the scene Ezra is laying punch after punch down on Rafe who looks to be struggling with the blocks. Not even I can get him to stop as I scream and beg, but after he lays a kick into Rafe's gut, I ambush him, tearing him away with every bit of strength I can muster. As he looks back at me, there is betrayal in his eyes.

There is no more crowd or boxing ring. It's just my brother beating my boyfriend within an inch of his life, but all he sees is me picking Rafe over him.

When they finally yell for him to freeze, he stops. Putting his bloody fists up, the cops are quick to ambush him. A moment later, he's in cuffs.

Gritting my teeth, I run over to Ezra who's now wearing a steeled expression with his lips pressed into a tight line and his eyes glazed over, facing forward in the back of the patrol car.

"I'm going to go post your bail right now."

"The judge won't be there until the morning. Go home, Shelby," he says flatly. Tears start to spring out of my eyes and down my cheeks.

"I can't just leave you," I cry, but he looks at me without emotion.

"I'm sorry," he whispers before the cop closes the

door and hauls my twin away.

It feels as if I can't breathe or think for a long time. How did this happen? He was just supposed to have a match with Rafe, and I honestly thought that would be the worst thing to happen tonight.

Rafe is still lying on the ground, alone, when one of the officers calls for an ambulance on his radio and kneels down next to Rafe.

By the time Rafe starts coming to, Ezra has been read his rights and is in the back of the patrol car. It feels like a cold brick laying on my chest, seeing him in police custody again. His eyes don't leave me as they start to haul him away.

Dropping down next to Rafe, I feel his pulse and touch my hand to his forehead. He presses his hands to the ground and pushes up. As he shifts to sitting, I see the deep, bleeding cuts to his lip and brow.

"Slow down," I say, putting a hand on his shoulder before he can stand.

"What are you doing here?" he asks, and I think he's talking to me at first, but then his eyes meet the officer standing next to him.

"We got a call about noise. I told Hopkins to call you first, but you weren't answering. This crowd was huge, Rafe."

"Fuck," he groans, then his eyes drift around the lot. His gaze finally meets mine when he asks, "Where's Ezra?"

"He's under arrest for assaulting an officer," the officer replies.

"Oh, my God," I blurt out. That's a serious offense, and suddenly I'm eager to run to the station to be with him. Surely they understand it was a consensual fight.

"It was a boxing match, Griff. Let him the fuck go."

"That didn't look like a boxing match, Rafe. It looked like assault."

"It was just a little amateur boxing. I'm not pressing charges, and I'm fine. Cancel the medic and turn the other patrol around, okay."

"And the chief? You'll handle him too?" The officer next to him asks dryly.

The one he called Griff steps closer to Rafe, and I'm close enough to hear the words he whispers. "You could lose your job for this, Rafe. We've turned our back long enough, but if you intervene with this arrest, it'll cost you your job."

Rafe looks pained at the thought. He glances at me again, and I can't hide the pooling tears in my eyes. "I'll handle it at the station, then."

He touches my back, and I snap. Spinning to face him, everything from the past month...from the past ten years all comes spilling out of my mouth.

"You did this!" I scream through my clenched teeth. "You wanted him arrested. You always wanted him gone, but he's my brother, Rafe!"

He doesn't speak, even as I slam my fists against his chest. I'm filled with so much anger, I want to hurt him. I could hurt him.

"You had his shop searched. You could have stopped this fight, but you didn't!" I cry.

"I didn't make that call," he mutters, but it's not enough.

"I signed the affidavit for search. The judge must have issued the warrant. I was so busy with everything that I didn't even notice. If I had, Shelby…"

"No!" I scream. Crumbling against his chest, I lose myself in the sobs that wrack my body.

He doesn't fight me or stop me from touching him, even as my nails scratch his skin. He just holds me as I cry.

"I'm going to fix this," he mumbles against my head. "Let me take you home, Shelby. You can't drive like this. First thing in the morning, I will fix this."

"The ambulance is on the way, Rafe. You have some serious cuts on your face," one of the officers says.

"Cancel it. I'm fine," he argues.

Without an answer, he pulls me to the parking lot. I make him let me drive my car, and we leave his bike parked in the empty lot. It doesn't even register to me that it's not a safe place to leave a motorcycle like that, but he doesn't seem to care. I don't speak to him the entire way home. I let my tears fall. Thinking of Ezra being processed at the station, getting a mugshot, sitting with those criminals, going through all of it again, it all breaks my heart into two.

How could I let this happen? He told me to get close to Rafe to get revenge, but somehow, we ended up at the bottom again.

Looking over at the man in the driver's seat, I can't find it in me to hate him again, no matter how hard I try. I know deep down he didn't mean to hurt me, but I'm still so angry with him, I want to hurt him. This love and anger I'm feeling is tearing me in two.

When we get the apartment, he stands awkwardly at his door, waiting to see where I'll go. At this point, I know I'm not making clear, smart decisions. The heavy weight of these emotions has made me numb, and I feel half-alive as I push into his apartment.

Desperate for something to wake me up, I walk into his kitchen to pour myself something to drink. He's watching me from the counter as I swallow down the glass of wine in one long gulp, burning my throat as it goes down.

Without speaking, he stands between me and the bedroom. The look on his face is apologetic and pitiful. My heart is shattering for him, through all of his pain and his trauma, but once again, I've walked into my own. Because of him, I'm hurting again, and it feels so fucking unfair to love someone who does nothing but hurt you. I don't hate him for it. I hate myself.

"I need to bandage those cuts," I mumble, moving toward my apartment to get the first aid kit I have there.

He grabs my arm. "I'm fine."

"No, you're not," I answer firmly. Yanking my arm free, I go to get my stuff and come back to him sitting at the kitchen table waiting for me. I clean his cuts in silence, and he watches me while I work. My brother did this to his face. Regardless, I'm still mad at him. And by the uneasy way he's watching me, he can tell I'm angry.

After the two cuts on his cheek and brow are bandaged, I walk toward the kitchen to pour myself another drink. I should really go back to my apartment, but I feel stuck here, like I don't remember how to be on my own.

The black silk rope hanging from the back of the chair catches my eye. Without a word, I walk toward it, letting the soft fabric run through my fingers.

"Do you know what this feels like?" I ask him. "To be tied up? To trust someone so much you give yourself over to them completely?"

"No," he answers, and I hear the strife in his tone. I know he's beating himself up for what happened to Ezra.

Settling my gaze on his face, I drown in those dark eyes before speaking. "Take your shirt off, and put your hands behind your back."

There's hesitation. He's afraid. Not of what I'll do to him but what it will feel like to give up control. To trust me.

Whether or not he should.

Finally, he pulls his shirt over his head and his hands move toward his back, and I walk behind him. He doesn't flinch as I wrap the rope around his wrists, tying it like I learned to do. The moment I have his hands bound, I feel the power over him that he felt over me.

I could hurt him. Humiliate him. Ruin all of the progress he's made to heal the scars from his childhood. He would never trust again.

As I walk around to face him, his eyes stay trained on my face. They are glassed over, and his chest is moving heavier. Is that desire or fear?

Softly, I drift my fingers down his chest, tracing the shape of his black and white tattoos across his skin. He flinches, his breathing hitching every few seconds.

Leaning forward, I press my lips to the center of his chest. His breathing stops entirely, and I rest my face there for a moment, feeling his heartbeat, now racing because of me.

He presses his lips against the top of my head, and I can tell he wants to touch me. There is a struggle against the rope, but he won't be able to get his hands out. This is what it was made for. If he wasn't truly powerless, it wouldn't have the same effect.

I trail my lips upward to his neck, tasting the sweat dried on his skin. He moves to find my lips with his, but I pull away. I'm teasing him, and I know it's a sweet, delicate torture.

My fingers move to his belt, pulling it off slowly, watching the way it makes him squirm with anticipation. Then, I move the button and zipper, never taking my mouth off of his body as I do.

Biting his shoulder, I reach into his boxers to hold his thickness in my hand. He sucks in a painful sounding breath through his teeth, matching my bite to the tightness of my grip.

"Shelby," he moans against my hair.

The surrender in his voice sends a shockwave through my heart. This is the first time I have outright held him in my hands, and it's too soon for him. He still has so much trauma to work through, and this could only be making him worse. I want to take my pain out on him, but I can't hurt him—not like that. I don't release him, but I soften my hold. Tears I had been holding back start to pool. "Do you want me to stop?"

There's a beat of silence.

"Do whatever will make you feel better," he says quietly. As my eyes drift up toward his, he stares firmly at me as he says, "I'm yours."

Feeling my sense of power return, I pull him over to the couch as he steps out of his pants. He's completely naked as I push him down, his painful looking erection pointing up toward me.

He watches me as I pull off my clothes, his eyes lingering over my breasts after I unclasp my bra, dropping it to the floor. As I climb on top of him, I keep my eyes on his face.

"Kiss me here," I tell him, pointing to a spot above my breast. He obeys, leaning forward to press his warm mouth against my skin.

"Lower," I command. My head falls back as his tongue glides over my nipple.

"The other one," I gasp and again, he obeys.

He listens to every command until I have his kisses stamped on every inch of my skin. Grinding myself on the length of his cock, I've soaked him with my arousal. Finally, I lift up and settle myself on top of him, sliding him in until we are fully joined. Shivers erupt along my spine as he fills me up.

His mouth parts, and his breathing hitches, and I know he's trying not to express his pleasure. This moment is mine, and he's surrendering it to me. Looping my arms around him, I bury my face in his neck as I grind my hips on him.

I've never been so in control during sex before. Squeezing his shoulders to the point where I know it must hurt, I move almost violently on top of him. Leaning back, still holding tightly to him, I see the pinnacle of my pleasure and I race toward it, erasing every single thought in my mind. My orgasm is building quickly as I move, picking up speed and slamming myself against him, finding the spots that send bolts of lightning through my body.

He lets out a heavy groan just as my climax takes over, and I match his cries with my own. It's a short but intense orgasm, so intense my limbs tingle and go numb as my body relaxes, melting against him.

With my face against his chest, the emotion I pushed away comes flooding back, and I begin to sob again. I don't know what I'm crying for. My brother, Rafe, for myself. For the intensity I feel toward him no matter how much I don't want to. How scared it makes me feel to care about him this much.

"Please untie me now so I can hold you," he begs, and I reach behind him, pulling the rope that allows it to unravel. In a rush, he wraps his arms around me, swallowing me against him, and it only makes me cry harder.

We can't come back from this. I wanted to help

him, and I thought it could just be sex, but my heart has changed. It cannot be unchanged. I don't want to stop helping him, and I don't ever want him to stop holding me.

"I wish I still hated you," I sob, my tears soaking his skin.

He kisses my head, whispering words that cut all the binds holding us a part. "I never hated you."

Chapter Twenty

RAFE

After a long, quiet shower together, I take Shelby to bed. I'm afraid she won't sleep because she turns her body away from me in the bed, and I stroke her back to help her relax. Finally, after almost an hour, her breathing slows, and I'm able to rest my hand.

I don't know how the fuck this all happened. We started this as a vendetta, but we opened something we can never close again. I wanted to be rid of her so I could live my miserable life in peace. Now, I can't bear to think of my life without her. I don't want to let her go. But if I don't make this right with Ezra, she may never be able to look at me the same way again.

The next morning, she's still asleep when I slide out of bed to make coffee. She finds me in the kitchen fifteen minutes later.

"I have to get to the station," she mumbles. "I called into work."

There are heavy bags under her eyes from the crying last night. "Let me take care of it. I'll post his bail. They've let a lot of rich kids slide around here for much less. I know the right people to talk to. For now, you try to get some rest."

"I have to go, Rafe," she mumbles, leaning on the counter. For a long moment, I just stare at her. With those golden bronze curls framing her face, she looks far too beautiful and pure for me. But I know this girl is tough as nails and doesn't just take shit without a fight.

"Then we'll go together." I touch her arm, but she doesn't warm up toward me. Instead, she moves toward the door.

"I'm going to go shower. Meet me outside in twenty minutes."

Once we get to the station, I talk to the clerk and make a few calls to get Ezra's bail down to only a hundred bucks, which I pay on the spot. It takes about an hour of waiting for them to do the paperwork, and only because I'm there to rush it along. As Ezra comes out, he gives us both a blank expression. He looks exhausted, too tired to even show me how much he hates me. He does admire the bright blue shiner on my face though.

No one says a word on the ride back to the apartment. Ezra sits silently in the backseat, staring out the window. In a weird way, it feels like old times, the three of us together again. I just wish it were under very different circumstances.

We will get through this, I tell myself. I almost reach across the console to hold Shelby's hand, but her cold expression stops me. I sure as fuck don't think that's what Ezra wants to see, so I don't.

Glancing into the rearview mirror, I make eye contact with Ezra. There's a silent conversation between us as we stare at each other. I glance over at Shelby for a moment, and I know he's thinking the same thing. What we did last night was stupid. It hurt the one person neither of us wanted to hurt, and all because we're hot-headed assholes who know how to hold a grudge. I wish it would have landed me in jail right next to him.

Once we get back to the apartment, I stop in front of my door as Shelby unlocks hers for Ezra. As much as I want to be near her right now, they need their space.

"Ezra, go use my shower and get some rest. I'll be in in a minute."

He doesn't say a word, which is very unlike him, as he does as she says. My heart actually starts racing, like I should be glad she wants to be with me. She follows me into my apartment, and we both notice the rope still lying on the floor where we left it last night.

I move to hold her in my arms, but she doesn't come closer. I swallow down the bad feeling stirring around in my gut.

"Rafe," she whispers while nibbling on her bottom

lip and tears pool in her eyes.

"It's been a long couple of days, Shelby. Why don't you go get some rest and focus on your brother for a bit."

"What you two did last night opened my eyes to the way things are between us. Then, what you and I did last night…" A choked sob escapes her lips.

"The fight was stupid. I'm sorry. You know how fucking sorry I am."

"It's more than just the fight, Rafe. It's everything. You're in self-destruction mode, and I don't want any part of it."

"Shelby," I say, and it comes out as a warning. If I ordered her to stop talking and tie me up like she did last night, would she obey?

"We need space, Rafe. I need time to think, and you just need to figure out what you want."

"I want you," I say, and even I don't believe the words coming out of my mouth. I mean of course I want her, but these are baseless words. I'm basically begging her to trust me to change, but we both know I'm not really going to. I will refuse help, resort to violence, and beg for forgiveness again and again.

"Then show me," she cries, finally looking up at me, tears falling across her cheeks.

I have nothing left to say as she turns and walks out of my apartment. The emotion is heavy on my chest, and I know it would be easy to play the poor me card and even as I reach for my gym bag, I stop. I can't punch my way out of this.

SHELBY

Ezra is still in the shower when I get back to my apartment, and thank god for that. Because I can't seem to stop crying. So I walk out to the patio, praying that Rafe doesn't do the same thing. Living next door to each other and avoiding each other should be interesting, but we need this. I knew after watching him get in the ring with my brother that things with him would never be healthy. I could love him as hard as possible, and it wouldn't be enough to fix what was broken. That part was up to him.

He had trauma to work through, trauma that festered for decades. I just prayed he would because the thought of him going back to the way things were, alone and angry, made my heart hurt. I meant what I said... we need a break, but if Rafe can't do what needs to be done, then it will be forever, and these are the thoughts that keep the tears falling.

I realized as him and I had sex on the couch last night, him giving me the control that I loved him, and perhaps I always had. And I told myself that him letting me tie him up was a good sign, if only I had done it for the right reasons.

I did it to hurt him. And that broke me.

So he's not the only one who needs to make some changes.

When I hear the bedroom door open, I turn and see Ezra coming out in some fresh clothes that he leaves in my apartment in case he sleeps over. I brace myself for this conversation because I suspect it will be even harder than the last one.

His face is still so sadly blank. Even as I walk inside and hand him a glass of water, he holds no emotion. It's probably not going to stay that way.

"We need to talk," I whisper. His jaw clenches.

"Will you let me apologize?"

"Of course, but I don't think it's going to change anything. Not right now."

"What are you talking about?" he asks, his face contorting into a look I recognize from the kid I knew growing up. When we were children and would fight over the smallest things. Things were never fair according to Ezra, and i have a feeling he won't find this fair either.

"I don't want to see you for a while, Ezra."

"Shelby," he snaps, and I wince. Pushing my only family away feels like ripping off a piece of my body. Am I worried that Ezra will do something terrible because I'm pulling myself out of his life? Yes, but he needs this. And so do I.

"You've been lying to me. Going to Chief's was not smart, Ezra. Fighting with Rafe over me? You've been holding onto so much rage and anger for too long, and you've pulled me into it. It's not fair, and I think we both need some space to clear our heads."

His mouth is hanging open and I spot moisture in his eyes.

"You're choosing him over me," he cries, and I shut

my eyes. Ezra will choose the offence over the defense every time.

"I'm not choosing him. I'm taking a break from both of you. You're both toxic, Ezra. And I'm finally choosing myself for once in my life."

His mouth closes, and I watch him fight off the urge to cry.

"I'm sorry," he begs, but I don't respond.

"I'll drive you home."

As I move toward my purse, he doesn't budge. "You're my sister, Shelby. You're all I have."

"You'll be fine, Ezra." Then before either of us can say anything else or I let him beg me to the point that I change my mind, I open the door and wait for him to walk through it.

It takes him a moment to realize that I'm being serious. I'm not going to change my mind. It's tough love, but I'm doing what I should have done years ago.

Chapter Twenty—one

RAFE

It's been eight days since Shelby last spoke to me, and it's been just as awful as I expected it would be. I hear her when she comes and goes, and I do my best to avoid running into her in the hallway. I work late, but I'm still not anywhere near productive. So when I finally get called in by the chief, I actually start to wonder what the hell took so long.

For the most part, he's a pretty laid back guy. He gives me a lot of free reign, maybe too much, but he knows how passionate I am about my job. He knows the basic summary of my upbringing but if he knows the nitty gritty he hasn't brought it up. As I step into his office, I keep my chin high and have a seat across from him. I know exactly what he's about to say.

At least I think I do.

"No more fighting, Nolan," he says with a heavy sigh as he places his hands on the desk and leans back to stare at me.

"Yes, sir," I answer. I haven't been to Vic's since last week, and I don't have plans to go back. In my head, quitting fighting is enough. Shelby told me to stop fighting my way through life, so I figure that's what I'm doing, but by the way the chief is staring at me, like there's a lot more he's about to say, I get the feeling that just giving up fighting won't be enough. Not for him, and not for her.

"I should apologize, son," he says, and my eyebrows furrow. Apologize for what?

But before I have to ask, he continues. "I'm putting you on administrative leave for thirty days."

My skin starts to grow hot, tingling from the crown of my head and down. He can't be serious.

"Sir."

He puts up a hand. "And mandatory anger management counseling."

That's when the anger changes to shame. I've been out of control for too long. I let it get out of hand. If I had just kept things quiet, this wouldn't have happened. I can't go to counseling. They'll see my record. They'll want me to open up a lot of shit that should not be opened.

"I can't do that, sir."

"I had a feeling you'd say that. Listen, Rafe." He

leans forward, and I know by the way he uses my first name that he's about to say something personal and probably pretty fucking uncomfortable. "You think I haven't seen your file? Of course, I have. But son, this isn't a punishment."

"I'll never get off admin leave. You know that."

"No, I don't. I know that I let it slide for too long. I wasn't doing you any favors by letting you struggle out there when I had the resources to help you."

My hands are starting to shake, so I clench them together. "I have work to do, sir. I'm in the middle of an investigation."

"The kid gave us the names we needed, Rafe. The DA cut him a deal. His charges have been reduced and all he had to do was give us a couple names. The DEA took over the case, and they've already made the bust in Newport. The case is closed, Rafe."

My mind takes a moment too long to process this information. Mateo came down to the station? Why didn't I know about this?

"His charges have been reduced?" I ask. For some reason, it's all I need to know.

"Misdemeanor. They offered the family protection, to move off Wickett, but they declined it. Said they feel safe here."

My head drops to my hands. Why would they do that? Why wouldn't they just take the protection?

"I wouldn't worry too much. The operation, according to the DEA, was amateur. More than anything, they just wanted to scare the kid, but he's fine."

I had Ezra's shop raided for this case. I believed it was him, and I was so hell-bent on this personal grudge that I let the real guys go for weeks. I wasn't there when Mateo needed me. I've let everyone down.

I need help.

Just letting those three words float through my mind feels like lifting a weight off my shoulders. I need fucking help so that I don't let this shit happen again. So I can live my life despite what my parents did to me instead of letting it control every ounce of good that comes.

"This will be for the best," the chief says, leaning forward. "You're a good cop, Officer Nolan. I can't afford to lose you."

Peeling my head up, I look across the desk and I try to see the good cop in my actions. Did I help Mateo? Have I helped anyone since I got the badge? Shelby asked me that when I first landed on her doorstep. Cops are supposed to help people, and what was I doing?

When it all started, I did. I made a difference in a few lives, in Theo's name. I didn't want anyone to go through what we did when Murph found his body. I knew that meant more than just putting a few dealers behind bars. If anyone knew about outliving our past, it was me. It's why I wanted to help Mateo, and why I knew I needed to make things right with Ezra.

I want to be a good cop again.

SHELBY

Life becomes a repetitive cycle of work, sleeping, and eating. I'm just going through the motions at this point. I haven't seen one trace of Rafe since the "break-up" if that's what you can call it. Even when I sneak down into the gym to get in a couple quick workouts between work and sleep, he's never down there, and the things are always exactly where I left them.

If I didn't hear his motorcycle pulling in late every night, I'd be worried he was dead in there.

When I have a day off, I find myself lying in bed, binging on Netflix and feeling pretty disgusting. My laptop dings somewhere in the middle of my Witcher binge, and I open it up to find a new email from Jillian. My heart nearly stops when I read it.

Sorry it took me so long. Here is that file you requested for your patient. ;)

"No, no, no, no," I mutter. I texted her and told her not to get it. I didn't want to see this, but she got it anyway.

Quickly, I shut my laptop. I shouldn't look at it. It's not none of my business. Plus, Rafe already told me everything. What good could it possibly do to look at it?

None.

I should just delete it. Opening up the laptop, I move toward the trash button, but I think about the little boy in that file. The abused boy who grew into a broken man. A broken man I love so much it hurts.

My mouse lingers over the file before I double-click it open. Chewing on my lip, I scroll through the paperwork. Seeing his name on these documents makes everything so real.

I can't read it. Not word by word, but there are phrases that stick out.

Physical abuse. Blunt force trauma. Second-degree burns. Emotional abuse.

The one that stops me in my tracks is Violent response to physical touch.

I slam it closed again. Closing my hand over my mouth, I muffle my own screams. I want to walk next door and hold him. I want to prove them wrong. He doesn't react violently to physical touch anymore. He is not broken, and this doesn't define him. My mind goes back to the man who rode me around the island on his motorcycle, who could make me laugh, bring me pleasure, who saved a woman's life for no other reason than because he could.

Instead of going next door, I lay my face down in my bed and cry. I can't fix him and going next door would only undo everything. It's up to Rafe and Ezra to fix their own problems, to heal themselves of this toxicity that's ruining their relationships. It just feels so unfair that I'm the one to pay the price.

During the day, Vic's gym looks like any other gym. There are paying customers working out and a boxing match going on with an instructor in the middle of the building. I see Vic right away when I walk in. He's standing at the back of the building talking with someone who looks like a plumber or handyman.

The light from the front door grabs his attention, and his face lights up as I walk in. Leaving the man he's talking to, he rushes over to greet me. Glancing around the room, I keep an eye out for Rafe, but I don't see him anywhere. I doubt he'd be here during the day anyway, but I'm still paranoid about it.

"What do I owe the pleasure, sweetheart?" He asks with that dangerous smile.

"I need your help," I say, holding my purse tighter. Nerves start to flood my brain as I look at him. I'm here, alone. I trust Vic, but for no other reason than he's been nice to me. For all I know, he could be just as bad as the rest of them.

"I would love nothing more than to help you, but I haven't seen your boyfriend all week."

"This isn't about him," I answer, straightening my shoulders. "It's about me."

"Okay..." he says, looking skeptical.

I clear my throat. I feel like an idiot, but this is what I want, and Vic is the only person, outside of Ezra and Rafe, that I trust to help me. "I want to learn how to fight."

His eyes squint ever so slightly, and his lips tilt in a small smile, almost as if he doesn't believe what I'm saying. "Like a self-defense class," he replies, stating it like a fact instead of a question.

"No. Like a boxing class. I want to learn how to

fight like a real boxer. No backdoor lot stuff either. The real thing."

Finally, his face breaks out in a grin from ear to ear. "Oh baby girl, I thought you'd never ask."

Chapter Twenty-two

RAFE

Six months later

Murph and I round the third mile, and I get to the point in our daily runs where I start to tell him how much I fucking hate him. Murph is bigger than me, older than me, and even though he's only been a dad for a few months now, he's starting to soften up and grow into his "Dad bod." Nevertheless, he kicks my ass on these daily jogs.

But in his defense, running was always his outlet. It's only been mine for three months.

This was what Dr. Hightower wanted, and I hated

to give him what he wanted, but I have to admit, they help. Other than the occasional boxing workout, I don't fight anymore. The last man I punched was Ezra. And I'd like to keep it that way.

We pass two ladies about ten years younger than us in nothing but sports bras and tiny shorts. They smile and wave as we pass, and I glance over at Murph who only shakes his head.

"A year ago you wouldn't have been shaking your head," I tease him.

"Yeah, well now all I can think is that if I catch Charlie jogging in that when she's their age, I won't let her leave the house."

Charlie is only four months old, and she's already got Murph growing gray hair. She's not even my kid, and she's changed all of us. Sierra's looking at Logan with stars in her eyes that scream baby fever now, and I've grown to a whole new level of protectiveness. We were already a family, but bringing in a kid...we've grown closer than ever.

"You know..." Murph says as he finally slows to a walk (thank God), "you could turn back and get one of their numbers. Or both, whatever."

"Pass," I answer quickly.

"It's been six months, man. You have to get back out there. You're not getting any younger, and the doc said you're clear to start new relationships. Give it a shot."

"He said I was clear to start slow. Plus...those girls don't look like what he was referring to." I nod back at the two blondes who are now long gone.

Murph laughs. As we reach the boardwalk, we stop into the shop and I can tell there's something else on Murph's mind. He tosses me an ice cold water bottle from the fridge in the back of the break room.

"If you're holding out for her, that's fine, but don't wait forever."

"Where is this coming from?" I ask, throwing up my arms. Murph isn't exactly the talkative type, especially when it comes to feelings, you know, like love. Logan is the young, poetic one.

"It's coming from knowing you my whole damn life, and never seeing you as happy as you are right now. And i know it's the therapy and all the quality time with me, but I think you did all this for her. I just don't want to see it all go to waste. I'm telling you this as a recovering asshole myself. I don't want to see you alone anymore. That's all I'm saying."

Things get heavy and silent for a minute, and after the last six months of heavy conversations and depressing stories from my past, I don't want to be so serious anymore. A lot of good has come from the conversations we've had, but I'm ready to get back to the brothers we used to be.

"Thanks, man," I answer, tossing back the ice cold water. "But for what it's worth, you're still an asshole."

On my way from Murph's shop, I stop by the souvenir shop, like I always do. Mateo is there, opening the store when I walk up.

He only has a few more weeks before he leaves for

college, so I try to stop in as much as I can. When I walk toward the counter to greet him, I spot someone coming out of the stock room, and I stop in my tracks.

Ezra is in business attire, brown slacks and a white linen button-up. He looks to have bulked up a bit since I saw him last. The dark circles are gone from under his eyes, and he has new ink peeking out of his short sleeves.

He freezes when he sees me, and it's silent in the shop for a long moment.

"Hey," he says finally.

"Hey."

He moves toward the front and gives Mateo a register full of cash and a spreadsheet to sign. They go along with their business, and I almost leave, feeling uncomfortable. But Ezra and I are in the same room without killing each other, and I kind of want to see how much farther I can take this.

When they finish talking, Ezra turns toward me. "Hey, can we talk a second outside?"

"Of course," I reply. A part of me considers reverting to my old ways. Defensive, violent, easily provoked. Instead, I wave goodbye to Mateo and walk outside to wait for him.

As he emerges from the store, Ezra shuffles uncomfortably in front of me before he finally speaks. Dr. Hightower always says the uncomfortable conversations will pay off ten to one, and after today, I hope I have ten years of good fortune.

Finally, he clears his throat. "How is she?" he asks,

and I have to think for a moment before responding.

"Shelby?"

"Yeah, of course Shelby. I just want to know that she's okay. I mean, she checks in every once in a while, but I haven't really spoken to her, and that fine, but—"

"Wait a minute," I interrupt him. "You haven't seen Shelby in six months?"

In my pocket, my phone starts buzzing, and mindlessly, I silence it.

Ezra's eyebrows twist in confusion. "Are you two not still together?"

"Still together? I haven't seen her since I last saw you."

My phone buzzes again.

"Neither have I," Ezra replies with regret written all over his face.

"Fuck," I mutter.

"It's okay," he adds. I know why she did it, and it was for the best. I've actually had time to get my shit together. You know...grow up and take care of myself for a change."

I let out a laugh, not because it's funny but because I know the feeling.

"Yeah, me too."

My stupid fucking phone is buzzing again, and I'm about to toss it into the ocean. As I pull it out, Ezra keeps talking, saying something about me and Shelby and how he thought we were the real thing, but I'm too busy reading the words on my screen. I hate being rude, but my mind can't possibly register what I'm looking at.

"Everything okay?" he asks, and I look up at him.

"No, it's fucking not."

SHELBY

Of course he decides to go today. Mr. Yan held on for six months, shocking the hell out of all of us, but on the most nerve-wracking day of my life, I got the call from Mrs. Yan at 5:15 this morning.

The house is quiet when I show up. I walk right in and find the rest of the family exactly where I left them last night. His daughter and grandkids sit huddled on the couch, their tears dried and sad smiles greeting me.

I wave at them before going into the living room where Mrs. Yan holds her husband's lifeless hand. Painful tears prick behind my eyes as I watch them. Slowly I walk over and she greets me with a warm smile as she takes my hand.

Gently, I reach down and touch his face. He looks so peaceful, and surprisingly, so does Mrs. Yan.

"He's not in pain anymore," she whispers. Then, she surprises the hell out of me, and she hugs me toward her body. Mrs. Yan has hardly even touched me in the entire time I've been here. I assumed she hated me, but still with all the time I've been coming around, we've become like family. They have kept me over for dinner, and I was here Christmas morning, Santa hat and all.

So, it's no surprise when my eyes start to mist over

and I realize how much I'm going to miss his smile. When he took a turn for the worse, I prepared myself. But he shocked us all and stuck around for so much longer. Part of me thinks that he must have known what a hard time I was going through then. I lost my boyfriend and my brother. I had to start navigating my life alone and for myself. It's a selfish thing to think that he held on, in pain, for me, but it's almost fate that on the day that all of my training has led to tonight he decides to leave me.

"He loved you," Mrs. Yan says to me, squeezing me tighter.

"I loved him too," I answer.

"Then you better not be a stranger now."

"Promise."

From then, I go through the procedure of checking his vitals one last time, just to confirm, and then I call the medical center that will be taking his remains. Mr. Yan donated his body to science, because of course he did.

I spend the next few hours with the family, which is not something I usually do, but today was supposed to be my day off and since I don't' have to be at the gym until four, I have the time. We sit around and drink coffee and eat the casseroles everyone has brought over, and for the first time ever, I feel like I'm part of a real family. I feel welcome.

And then I think of Rafe.

I should tell him about my match. I should, but I don't. I don't know why, but it's just been so long since we last spoke that I'm afraid he's moved and probably wouldn't care anyway.

I also don't tell Ezra because I don't want him getting all worked up about it. Tonight is about me, and what I've trained for. He'll just get mad or try to talk me out of it. They both would.

So I made a deal with myself instead. If I win tonight, I will call them both. I will mend what we broke six months ago, assuming they've changed.

If I lose, I'll keep at it. Keep fighting. This break wasn't just for them. It was for me too.

And if I have something to fight for, I stand much more chance of winning.

I'd be lying if I didn't admit that I have been watching them both a little. Rafe doesn't use the gym downstairs anymore, and according to Vic, he doesn't fight anymore either. Well, not here at least, since they officially shut down the illegal betting.

When I see him out the window as he gets off his bike, I notice the way his body has changed. He's filled out and his skin looks about three shades tanner from those early morning runs I've noticed he's been taking.

He's changed. I can tell, and he did it for me, so the least I can do is text him.

Chapter Twenty-three

RAFE

It wasn't just getting a text from Shelby that threw me off. It was the fact that I got six in a row, which would have been fine if the third one didn't outright say she would be fighting in a match at Vic's tonight.

Hey. I know this is out of the blue, but I hope you're doing well.

I didn't mean for that to sound so formal. I'm not good at this. For all I know you've completely moved on, and if that's the case, just completely ignore this.

Dammit. The whole point of this was to invite you to Vic's tonight. I'm having my first match. I've been training for six months, and I'm really nervous.

I mean, I know it'll be fine. I've worked hard. I'm not worried, just nervous, you know?

Anyway, I hope you can make it. No pressure. If you can, it'd be great to see you.

I miss you.

This can't be happening. Fighting at Vic's? Didn't she want me to stop fighting because that's what I did.

"What do you know about this?" I ask Ezra as I show him the texts. His eyes go wide as he reads through them.

"What the fuck?" he asks.

"We have to stop her," I answer, as I'm typing my response.

Tell me you're kidding.

Where are you?

You're fighting at Vic's over my dead body.

Ezra's too.

She's not answering. And soon Ezra and I both find that she's not home either. He follows me in his car as we rush over to Vic's. She's not there either.

When I find Vic, I fight the urge to put my fist through his teeth. I've changed. This isn't the guy I am anymore. But protecting Shelby brings out this caveman in me, and I can't help it.

I put up my hand as I burst through his office. "What the fuck is going on?" I ask, Ezra hot on my heels.

Vic responds with a hearty laugh. "I expected this. Took you long enough."

"How is this funny?" I grit through my teeth.

"Because you're predictable. She knew you'd react like this," he answers, closing his laptop.

"Well how else are we supposed to react?" Ezra adds from beside me.

Vic's smile fades as he looks at the man next to me. "If you weren't Shelby's brother, I'd have you dragged out of here by your teeth."

"Vic," I bark, bringing his attention back. "What do you expect us to do?"

He stands up and shakes his head at us. "I don't know, guys. Support her? Cheer her on? Has it occurred to either of you that she's a lot stronger than either of you give her credit for? I don't want to spoil it for you, but she's one of the strongest female beginners I've had in this club. She's the last one to believe it, but she's going to win tonight, hands down. So maybe instead of convincing her that she's not strong enough, come here and stand on the sidelines for her. God fucking knows she's done it for the both of you."

Well that certainly shuts us the fuck up.

I look over at Ezra and it's clear he's thinking the same thing. Vic is right. We've both put Shelby on the sidelines, expecting her to support us, accommodate us, sacrifice for us. And as much as it pains me to even think about it, I guess I'll be there to support her.

The fight starts at five, and when we meet back at the gym, Ez and I keep our eyes peeled for Shelby. I texted her back about ten times after I made an ass of myself with my first replies. I looked like a psychopath apologizing and spilling my heart over unanswered text messages.

The crowd is crazy tonight. The female fights surprisingly pull a big audience. I spot one of my exes, a bartender I haven't seen in years, and by the look she's sending me, she's not a huge fan of mine.

Ezra and I stand around with Vic, waiting impatiently for the matches to start. Vic meets us at the front of bleachers. He grabs me by the shoulder and points to the back of the gym where I see Shelby. I almost don't recognize her with her curls pulled back in a tight ponytail and her tight gym clothes in all black. She's pacing by Vic's office, listening to one of the female coaches who is talking to her.

I have to talk to her.

Just as that thought crosses my mind, she looks up and sees me. As our eyes meet, I remember every sappy thing I wrote in a text message today.

Everytime I thought I hated you, I was just masking the fact that you are the only person I love without needing you to love me back.

There wasn't a day in those ten years that I didn't think about you. That I didn't wish you had moved on without me.

I regret you got the broken version of me.

"I'll be right back," I mumble to the guys as I make my way toward her. In a panic, she turns away from me, and I don't want to get in her head before her fight, but I just want to do what Vic said I had to do: support her.

"Don't try to stop me," she snaps as I step up to her.

"I'm not," I say with a smile, putting my hands up.

"You're not?"

"Yeah, didn't you get my messages?"

She tilts her head with a twist to her lips. "Yes, then I turned off my phone."

A laugh suddenly escapes my lips. She didn't read any of my heartfelt texts. "What is wrong with you?" she asks.

"Nothing." I suddenly wish we hadn't spent the first minute of our reunion arguing, but I can't wipe the smile from my face. Now that I look at her, I see the new sculpted biceps and hardness to her stomach. She's been working hard. "I'm proud of you."

"Really? I thought you didn't want me to do this."

"I don't," I answer honestly as I place my hands on her shoulders. Just touching her again has me missing her even more. I miss her touch, the way it felt to nuzzle my face into her neck, her legs wrapped around me, her fingers as they glided across my chest.

"Then why are you here?" I feel the way she's leaning into me, and I almost break.

Leaning in, our foreheads almost touching, I whisper the words she never read in those text messages. "Because I missed you."

I thought she might let me kiss her. What I didn't expect was her to yank her face back and point her finger at me. "I have to win."

"Okay," I say, feeling a little confused.

"I can't kiss you unless I win."

My eyebrows dart up to the top of my head. "Well, that seems a little harsh."

She smiles up at me just as Vic calls her over and takes up to the ring.

"Shelby," I call for her just before she climbs up. She turns back to stare at me. "You better fucking win."

SHELBY

The girl walking toward me isn't any bigger than me, but she is staring at me like she wants to rip my face off. I swallow down my nerves and step into the circle. I sparred before but never with Isabel. She's young and tough as nails, but Vic feels confident that I can beat her.

He says she's feisty, but she doesn't think. Apparently, I have the brains and the strength to pull it off, but I can't seem to feel all of that confidence he wants me to feel.

Vic decides to take the ref job on this fight. After taking the mic and doing his announcer bit, he turns toward us and puts his hands out for each of us to put our wrists on his. "A fair fight, ladies. Yes?"

"Yep," she snaps. Then she holds her fists out toward me and I knock them quickly. Suddenly, at that moment, I stop feeling like Shelby, the nurse and quiet rule follower. I'm ready to fight, ready to get hit.

In the corner of my eye, Rafe is standing there, his arms crossed and a blank expression on his face. Beside him, Ezra is a ball of nerves.

I push the image of them aside. This isn't about them. It's about me.

When Vic rings the bell—an actual bell because he loves to be authentic—my opponent comes in quick with a swing on the left, and for a moment, I don't think. Nothing my coaches told me to do to prepare registers, and I just throw up my arms to block her. The impact of her punch on my arms hurts so bad. But quickly, my adrenaline spikes and the pain is replaced by a buzzing under my skin.

I watch her eyes, seeing where she is about to land her next punch, and I block her again. This time when she throws her punch, I follow with my own directly to the side of her face.

I have never honestly punched someone before this moment, and as a nurse, I honestly feel bad for how good it feels to slam my fist against her cheek.

She falters, and judging by the surprise in her round eyes, she didn't expect me to be so strong. The crowd around us erupts in cheers, and I see behind her where Rafe is watching, still stoic and calm.

Ezra on the other hand is hanging off Rafe's shoulders, shouting things at me that I can't even begin to register. Rafe signals something at me, pointing to his eyes then to her.

He's telling me to focus, but it's a little too late because her fist comes crashing against my face, sending me tumbling backward. I don't fall down, but I want to. It's not just the fact that it hurt, but that it was completely disorienting.

I see him again, and his calm demeanor keeps me grounded. With my fists back up and my elbows in, I move back toward the center.

Managing to block a couple more punches, I get in one more before the bell rings. Walking over to the corner where my coach is waiting, I don't take my eyes off Rafe. With the next breath, he's up and standing on the ring until he's face-to-face with me. I don't say a word as he grips my face in his hands. Inspecting a sore spot on my cheek, he pulls my face close.

"Turn everything off. Focus on the fight. You've practiced this enough. Let your body do what you've taught it to do."

For some reason, I want to cry. Tears start to spring to my eyes, and he notices it. He swallows, and I have to bite down on the mouth guard to keep from losing it.

"It's the adrenaline. Don't' worry about it," he mutters while Ezra bounces next to him.

But I want to tell Rafe it's so much more than adrenaline. It's him standing there, being my rock, the person I come to when I need someone to hold me up. It's the fact that seven months ago, we hated each other—or at least we thought we did. It's how broken we both were and how we both managed to find the one person worth being selfless for.

As the bell rings, he wipes the tears that have fallen. "Now, go kick her ass," he mutters before pushing me away.

The tears on my cheeks dry, and I focus only on the motion of her eyes as they land on my face. She goes in for another swing, landing a punch straight to my ribs, and the pain makes me want to vomit.

I keep letting her take all the swings, but mine are falling short. Everytime I make contact, it never feels like enough. Like I'm not putting my all into it.

By the next round, I feel myself slipping. I'm getting tired and worried that I'm not as confident to win as she is.

So by the fourth round, I get my water, look at Rafe who is now so wound up that I literally feel his energy radiating toward me. I know I need to end this now. I don't have it in me for five more rounds, and if I let her throw all the punches, I'm going to lose.

Shoving my mouth guard back in, I think about how good it's going to feel to kiss Rafe again and what I'm going to do to him when we get back to the apartment, and when I see her ready herself for another punch, I beat her to it, laying a cold left to her face, followed by a series of hooks that she never recovers from. I see Rafe screaming for me as I throw the last punch that sends her straight to the floor.

Chapter Twenty-four

RAFE

Ezra is practically on top of me as Vic drops to the floor to count. As he reaches the tenth count, I'm in the ring and Shelby is in my arms. There's blood trickling from her lips, and her skin is slick with sweat as I hoist her up, but I can't help it. I need this. And judging by the way she wraps her legs around my waist, she's okay with it.

"You're fucking amazing," I smile as she pulls my face in for a kiss. Quickly, she tears her gloves off and digs her fingers in my hair.

"Jesus," Vic mutters as he taps my shoulder. "Will

you get the fuck off of my figher so I can do this?"

"Oh yeah," she says as she jumps off my waist.

I back out of the ring to give her her moment when Vic crowns her the winner because I want her to feel that. She deserves it.

After she climbs down and back into my arms, I feel Ezra standing next to us.

"Shelby," he mumbles. Pulling away from me, she stares at him with a smile.

"Thank you for coming," she says before she wraps her arms around his neck.

"I'll give you two a minute." Then, I walk toward the back lot where the party would normally spill out to after the proper matches. Vic walks up behind me.

"I miss it," he says as he lights his cigarette.

"Yeah, sometimes, I do too."

I know what I miss is not the fighting, but the easy way I worked through my pain. It makes me laugh now when I think about how getting punched so hard I would see stars was easier than talking about my feelings, but it was honestly more painless.

"This girl is giving me ideas about this place. Bringing in youth MMA and that bullshit."

I let out a laugh. "She can be annoying like that." Then I glance at him, letting out a heavy sigh. "Listen, I'm sorry you got shut down. I'm glad they didn't take the whole gym."

He waves his hand at me. "Don't worry about it. I'm sorry you got a month's paid vacation for it."

"Hey," I bark in a warning, but he sends me that

charming Vic smile, and I just roll my eyes and go back inside to find Shelby.

After she showers and comes out ready to go, she agrees to let me take her home. It's not hard to bargain with her when I remind her that I brought my bike. With an easy smile, she agrees and latches onto my arm.

We both say goodbye to Ezra who lets his eyes linger on me a moment longer than I expect them to. Everything between us isn't healed. We still have a lot to recover, but tonight I remembered what it was like to have him as a friend.

As Shelby climbs on the bike behind me, I stroke her hands with mine, and she leans her face against my back.

"I missed you," she whispers just before I fire up the engine.

Suddenly I can't get her home fast enough.

SHELBY

It feels so good to have his body against mine as we ride through the night. After everything, we needed to get her, to this moment.

The adrenaline from the fight has worn off and it leaves me feeling exhausted, and I almost nod off a couple times on the ride. It felt so good to win, so good. It was like once I realized how much I deserved to win, I fought like it. Before that, I was selling myself short.

And if he hadn't been there to be my rock, I don't know if I would have.

When we get back to the apartment, we don't play the "whose apartment are we going to" game. He takes my keys and unlocks my door, leading me in and locking it behind us.

"I figured you want to be in your place after a fight," he says when he notices me watching. Honestly, I don't care what apartment we're in as long as we're together.

I already showered at the gym, so I don't need to shower here. Instead, I pour us both a glass of wine. But he only takes one sip before he sets it on the count and pulls my face in for a kiss. I love when he wraps his hands around my face like that, and I hum into the embrace. I missed it so damn much.

"I've been going to therapy," he mumbles against my lips.

My eyes pop open and I stare at him.

"I quit fighting, and I started running," he adds.

"Why are you telling me this?"

"Because you deserve to know. You made that happen for me."

Then, without warning, he pulls his shirt off his body, baring himself before he takes my hand and puts it on his chest. "I'm not perfect," he says, staring into my eyes. "I still have a long way to go."

Pulling my body closer to his, I whisper. "I'm so proud of you." I kiss him again, trying to savor the way his lips feel against mine. I am never letting him go again. I can't.

Without warning, he scoops me up, and I wrap my legs around him as he carries me to the bedroom. Our kiss is growing more heated as he lays me on the bed, ripping my clothes off in a rush until I'm lying beneath him completely naked.

His mouth trails from my neck down to my breasts while his hands skim up the length of my thighs until he reaches the pooling arousal between my legs. As he takes one of my nipples into my mouth, his finger glides into me, and I almost come undone from the contact. It's been so long since I've been touched, I practically die from the pleasure his fingers bring.

He nearly has me coming in minutes, but I pull his face off of my body to kiss him.

"I want you inside me. I don't want to come until you do."

In a rush, he pulls off his pants and lets his boxers drop to the floor. As he shifts our bodies up to the pillows, the tip of his cock finds the heat, teasing me for a moment before he slides in.

Having him back inside me is everything. It makes me think that this could be it for me. Rafe is all I want, and I will gladly spend the rest of my days with his mood swings and his rare smile, knowing every minute that he will be there for me. I want to spend the rest of my life with someone I trust and who I know trusts me.

Pressing himself to the hilt, his lips find mine again. Our breaths turn into pants and groans as he picks up speed, each slamming motion stronger than the one before. I won't take much longer, and when his hands find mine, intertwining our fingers, I let myself go. My body seizes itself in pleasure.

"Shelby," he howls as I feel his body jerk.

It is perfection, and for a long moment I can hardly breathe.

"I love you," he whispers as he collapses on top of me. His lips find my ear and I give those words back to him. I love you. I love you. I love you.

Chills run down my spine, and I know this is it. This is forever, and I know that we've already seen rock bottom. We have seen it all together. We have nowhere to go but up.

Epilogue

RAFE

"Easy on the throttle."

Mateo responds with something in Spanish as he speeds away on the custom ride Murph and I have been putting together all summer.

The kid is a natural, but it still makes me nervous as fuck to see him making turns around the empty lot. And I can see how hard he is on the clutch with every acceleration.

"I promised your aunt I wouldn't let you get hurt, but if you don't slow the fuck down, I'm going to whoop your ass."

Logan laughs behind me as he claps a hand on my shoulder. "You look like Theo when he taught me how to ride."

As Mateo circles back and comes to a stop in front of us, I tighten my jaw and try to force a deep breath into my lungs.

"I'm ready," he harps with a smile.

"You're not taking this thing with you to college." The barking command makes him smile.

"Yes, sir."

"And you only ride with me until you're twenty-one."

"Twenty."

Murph fires up his bike behind me. "Come on. We have to go meet the girls."

Letting out an exasperated groan, I get on my own bike and point at Mateo. "You stay between us the whole way."

He nods obediently, but he still has that smug grin on his face, and I know it means he's doing what I ask, but inside he's laughing at me. He thinks I'm being too protective, but I just gave an eighteen year old a custom-built motorcycle.

"He can't ride in that," Murph says as he tosses me the jacket I had Shelby sew the Wicked Beach patch on. I watch Mateo's eyes light up as I open it up for him. Logan, Murph, and I are wearing matching ones.

"The cool breeze on the beach can be brutal. You'll need this."

As Mateo slides it on his arms, I feel a strange tugging in my chest. A year ago, I would have slammed my fist straight into something to make it go away, but now I wear this new feeling with pride. Like a new patch on my sleeve.

I'm going to miss this kid when he's gone. And I'd be lying if I said that I didn't give him this bike as a way to ensure he had to come back and see me.

Dr. Hightower says that Mateo is my retribution. My concern and care for him is me "reappropriating my grief for Theo," and I hated that idea at first, but the more I let it sink in, the more sense it makes.

The four of us ride together back to the boardwalk where the girls are waiting for us on the pier. As we park the bikes, I look up to see Shelby sitting next to Savannah and holding Charlie in her arms. There's a bright smile on her face as she kisses the baby's bare belly making her break out in giggles.

It's doing things to me.

It's only been a month since we got back together, and we're taking things slow, but who wouldn't be daydreaming about a future with this woman.

But kids?

I shipped that idea off a long time ago. What if my trauma somehow gets passed down to my kids? What if my shitty lack of parental guidance makes me a terrible father?

I'm getting way the fuck ahead of myself right now. Shelby is still comfortably on the pill, and will be for a while. There isn't a doubt in my mind that she's mine forever. This is it for me, but how long until she starts thinking the same things I am.

The way she's glowing with that baby in her arms, she's already thinking them.

"Uh-oh," Logan laughs as he glares at my thousand-yard stare. "I know that look."

I shake my head at him as I climb off the bike and join the girls. Shelby smiles at me with Charlie in her arms. "Want to hold her?"

The words hell and no are on my tongue, but that was the old Rafe—the one made of stone and regrets, but as Charlie drools on Shelby's fingers, I let myself nod instead.

"Of course I do."

It's not like it's the first time I've held her. It is, however, the first time I've held her in front of Shelby. If I didn't want her to get ideas in her head, I would have said no. But maybe I want ideas in her head. Maybe I want her to imagine this is our baby, with her curls and my brown eyes, looking up at each of us like we hang the moon every night.

As she passes Charlie to me, I scoop her into my arms like a football, letting her hang facing forward and pressing my nose to the back of her head and inhaling that fresh new baby scent.

Shelby nibbles her cheek as he watches me, the smile she's trying to hold back reaching her eyes. I can feel the eyes of everyone around us, but I don't care. Shelby and I are the only ones who exist right now. Just her and me and all of these crazy ideas, like babies and a wedding and forever. Ideas that never stood a chance with the man I used to be.

SHELBY

Good lord, I had no idea watching your boyfriend hold a baby was such an aphrodisiac, but I can barely keep my hands off of Rafe. As we sit on the beach with all of his friends, my filthy mind is just running through all the ways I want him to fuck me when we get home so he can fill me up with that beautiful baby making seed.

I do not want a baby right now. That would be insane. Rafe and I still have so much to work out first. We haven't even fully moved in together yet. I mean, we never sleep alone anymore, but the actual moving in together step is serious.

But this is our future, and seeing how natural he was flying Charlie around the pier like she was an airplane, her arms and legs kicking in pure ecstatic joy, I knew that I wanted that.

And I want it with him.

"Please hurry home," I whisper after we say our goodbyes to everyone and climb onto his bike.

"Why?" he asks so innocently and I let out a low giggle in his ear as I grind my hips against him and reach my hand around to rub my hand at the zipper of his pants.

His spine stiffens and he glances back at me. "Oh, yes ma'am," he answers, and I laugh.

The baby thing plus the rumble from the bike, and I'm a very horny woman.

It's a good thing we live close to here. We barely

make it inside before I have his zipper undone. Quickly, I tear off my sundress and unclasp my bra until I'm in nothing but my panties. We don't make it to the bed and settle for his couch. As he drops down, I climb onto his lap, straddling him and kissing him so hard, he lets out a low groan.

Suddenly, his hand comes up with something in the corner of my vision.

"What do we have here?" he asks, and I let a wicked smile stretch across my face as I take in the long black ribbon sliding between his fingers.

"Turn around," he commands when he sees the lust in my eyes.

I do as he asks, and he binds my wrists with ease. Once, this was for him—a safe way for us to be together. But now, it's just fun. And it never fails to strengthen our bond. Trusting him so intensely not only turns me on, but it amplifies every emotion in my heart when he looks at me.

As soon as my arms are bound, he slowly peels down my underwear. I am fully naked in front of him while he is still dressed. It's a form of vulnerability and degradation that makes warmth pool between my legs. I squeeze my thighs together and wait for the next orders.

"Bend over."

He's still sitting on the couch behind me so that when I bend, I am exposed and bared for him. I thought we would be doing it quickly, but I can tell he wants to take his time with me now. And normally I'd want that too, but right now I only have one thought on my mind.

"I need you inside me," I groan as he glides his fingers along my sex.

"Oh yeah?" he moans, his lips against the skin of my backside. "You want me to fill you up?"

I let out a moan. "Yes."

In the next moment, he twists me around and flips me over his shoulder. Then he carries me to the kitchen table, my arms still tied together helplessly behind my back. As he places me down, he bores his lust-filled stare on me as he unzips his pants and his cock springs free.

"You want my seed in you?" he breathes as he grips me by the back of the neck, pulling my face close to his.

"Yes," I pant.

As he shoves himself inside of me, I squirm, loving the way I have to spread my knees even further to make room for him. "You want my baby growing in your belly?"

I don't so much as say yes as moan, "yes, yes, yes."

Picking up speed, he watches my face as he builds up momentum. Everytime I lose my balance, unable to hold myself up with my hands, it turns me on even more. I'm helpless, and he has to hold me up—my rock, my everything. Without him, I could not survive, and he knows it. This isn't just a game we play. It's the life we live. He needs to be needed, and although I've known life without him, I never want to know it again.

And as we both come together, shaking in mutual climax, we both pretend that I'm not on the pill and that what he's spilling into me would actually build a real future together.

For now, this is a fantasy.

But as he unties my hands and I collapse into his arms, I know we're both thinking about a very real future, and absolutely nothing is holding us back.

Also by Sara Cate

WICKED HEARTS SERIES
Delicate
Dangerous
Defiant

AGE-GAP ROMANCE
Beautiful Monster
Beautiful Sinner

WILDE BOYS DUET
Gravity
Free Fall

REVERSE HAREM
Four

COCKY HERO CLUB
Handsome Devil

About the author

Sara Cate writes forbidden romance with lots of angst, a little age gap, and heaps of steam. Living in Arizona with her husband and kids, Sara spends most of her time reading, writing, or baking.

You can find more information about her at www.saracatebooks.com

9 781956 830026